Book I

AND TIME STOOD STILL

D1520057

DEBBY LAWSON

To David's
mom
Sherry enjoy
Hope you
God Bless

Debby
Lawson

Edited by Jessica West

www.west1jess.com

Formatted by Drew Avera

www.drewavera.com/book-formatting

This book is dedicated to my husband Paul:
For always believing I had a story to tell, and,
For the inexhaustible encouragement he gave me to follow my dream.
Also
I want to thank my dear friend Carla, for reading each chapter as it was being written,
For without your interest and encouragement I may have never finished it!
And
Thank you to my sister Bonnie, my brother Larry and wife Faye for encouraging me always to tell my stories!
And last but not least
Thank you, Edna for editing my very first draft in 2015; thanks to my friends and beta readers
Maggie, Reba and Barbara for their feedback;
And, a special thanks to my daughter-in-law, Jessica West, for editing the final product
And, for giving me the support and confidence I needed to publish my first book

"The boundaries which divide life and death are at best shadowy and vague. Who shall say where one ends, and the other begins?"

-Edgar Allen Poe

CHAPTER ONE

"THE INTRODUCTION"

I averted my eyes and pretended not to notice the old lady struggling to come through the door of the medical center, hoping someone else would come to her rescue, but no one did. So, I got up from my chair and helped her in. Little did I know how that act of kindness to this stranger would forever change the scope of my life. She told me her name was Carine and thanked me for my help. I was happy to do it, so I gave her a smile and sat back in my chair. I planned to resume reading my book but to my dismay, she continued the conversation.

"Thank you so much for helping me. I'm all alone in this world, and I have no choice but to depend on the kindness of strangers."

"Oh, it was no problem at all," I said, knowing that my first reaction was to ignore her and the situation. I was raised catholic and we don't handle guilt well. I knew it was rude to not continue the conversation so I began making small talk.

"Do you live around here, Ms. Carine?"

"Yes, I live north about ten miles out of town, she replied in a sweet tone. What about you? Where do you live?"

"I live in the same direction."

"It sounds like we might be neighbors."

"Yes, it does," I said, *Great, we're neighbors. Here's hoping she won't just show up at my door.* I know, it's horrible to think this way, but my life was so busy and stressful that I had neither the time nor the energy to get involved with anyone else's problems.

The span of years between us was at least forty years or more. She had an elegant way about herself and dressed in a classic style. I could tell by her mannerisms that she had once been a charming and beautiful woman. She held herself with grace and authority even though her shoulders were bent with age.

I found myself curious to learn more about this woman, even as I asked myself why.

At that moment, the nurse appeared and called my name to go in for my appointment. I told Ms. Carine that it was nice meeting her and I wished her all the best. She had a smile on her face like she knew something I didn't know, and again thanked me for my assistance.

I couldn't stop thinking about her and wondering about her life. Her statement about being all alone bothered me. No one should be alone, especially at her age. Even in the midst of my misery, I felt sorry for her and regretted that I hadn't given her my number, just in case she needed help. After all, it seemed that we were neighbors. I shouldn't have worried, though, because when I came out of my appointment, the nurse handed me a note Ms. Carine had left for me.

The note read:

Dear Danielle,

I hope I'm not being intrusive but I would love to have you come over to my house for coffee. I will understand if you don't accept my invitation, but I hope that you do. I realize that I am an old lady, but I was young once and I haven't forgotten what that feels like. Here is my number. I hope that you will call and let me return your kindness.

Thank you,

Carine Dubois

My first reaction was nope, that is not going to happen. I stuffed her note in the bottom of my purse and left. I had so much going on in my life I couldn't consider spending my precious time visiting with someone I didn't know. But, I had to admit there was something intriguing about her, though I couldn't quite put my finger on it. That little voice in the back of my mind said, *what would it hurt?*

A couple of weeks went by. Things at work slowed down and I didn't feel so overwhelmed anymore. I thought about Ms. Carine and decided to call her and see if her invitation still held. I could hear the excitement in her voice when she answered, so we made plans to get together at her house for coffee that Saturday. She only lived a couple of miles from me, so her home should be easy to find.

I woke up to a stormy Saturday morning. I considered calling to cancel my visit but decided against it. I followed her instructions to find her home, and I couldn't believe that I never knew that road existed. This beautiful, narrow little road had an old wooden bridge that crossed over a muddy bayou with gigantic oak trees that lined both sides of the road, creating a canopy of darkness.

The trees were magnificent and their huge branches rested on the ground. Each branch was adorned with masses of moss hanging from them that reminded me of an old woman's tangled gray hair. The leaves on the branches were so thick sunlight couldn't penetrate them, creating a deep darkness against the stormy sky. When I reached the end of the road, I turned right and followed a narrow winding driveway lined with gravel, that led to a huge house a hundred years or older.

There was a pond in front of the house and another behind it. Both of the ponds looked unkempt, with long grass surrounding them. I shivered, thinking of the snakes that slithered in that tall grass, but was also thrilled because I love the character of old houses and the history behind them. I wouldn't have known the house— not visible from the road—existed at all if not for Ms. Carine's invitation. What a shame that would have been. Already I was glad to be there.

The house stood so proudly like a place frozen in time. It was a massive, two-story, wood-framed, plantation home with an Acadian style. It had a small set of stairs on the porch that led into the attic. The porch was wide and partially wrapped around the house with huge columns holding it in place. The old home was in disarray and in need of work. Some people would consider it a spooky place, but I could tell how grand she once had been.

In the distance, a wrought iron fence ran a short distance under a tree. *Surely that's not a graveyard.* The hair on my arms stood up. I started to walk there then stopped, realizing that to tour the grounds without first being asked would be rude. I would have to wait for an invitation. To the right of the house was an overgrown orchard with plum, orange, fig, and lemon trees.

A grove of pecan trees stood barely visible in the distance. An old brick pathway led around the house to the backyard. Once upon a time, this was a magnificent place.

Tendrils of ivy trailed up a wooden trellis on the side of the house, stopping just shy of the second floor. As I gazed up a child's face, a little girl perhaps, appeared in the upstairs window, but so briefly I wasn't sure I'd seen it at all.

Ms. Carine opened the front door and motioned for me to come in.

I glanced at the window once more, but saw only curtains. No faces and no motion. The crack of a lightning bolt close by sent me inside in a hurry.

Walking into this house was like stepping back in time. It took my breath away. Fourteen-foot high ceilings and a massive fireplace were the least impressive features. A magnificent set of stairs with a rail that was stained a beautiful red mahogany commanded the space. Obviously, a master craftsman had carved this work of art. The stair rail ended with the head of a mermaid, and the post below her had been carved into the shape of her body. Her arms, raised above her head, gave the appearance that she alone held up the stairway. The tail of the mermaid wound around the post.

I couldn't help but gasp when I saw her. She was beautiful; she looked alive. Her long hair, with its carved intricate curls cascaded over her breasts and hung below her waist.

In the end, it was her eyes that held my complete attention. They seemed to burn right through my soul and invoked feelings of emptiness and despair.

"Impressive, isn't she?" asked Ms. Carine.

"Yes," I replied. "I've never seen anything quite like it."

"No, and you never will," she said. "This house is over two-hundred years old and has always been in my husband's family.

"This stair rail was built by a slave named Aoesp. He was stolen from his family by slave traders at the tender age of six. He always told anyone who would listen that his father was a prince in his great country of Africa.

"He also said that it was his father's right-hand man who handed him over to the slave traders. I don't know if anyone ever believed him. He was so young, and he was known to have quite an active imagination. My husband's grandfather bought him straight off of the ship in New Orleans. He paid one hundred dollars for him, and that was a lot of money in those days. He was a frail boy, not able to work in the cotton fields, but he had a great mind and learned quickly.

"He was put to work with the carpenters, and began carving things. Aoesp was a born storyteller and entertained anyone who would listen to him. He believed with his whole heart that he once saw a mermaid when he was just a little boy.

"The memory of that day remained clear to him all the days of his life. He was collecting water for his mother and heard a low moaning sound coming from under a bridge made of sticks. He believed that someone was hurt, and he called out, 'Who's there?' There was no answer. With eyes widened in fear and dread in the pit of his stomach, his mouth went dry. He turned to leave when he heard it again. He had to see what was making this sound, so he walked over to the makeshift bridge.

"He couldn't believe his eyes. It was a woman, and her silver-colored hair was wrapped around the mess of sticks that made up the bridge's support. It was so tangled that her scalp was bleeding. She'd grown weak from struggling to break free. He could not stop staring at her because her skin was a pale green. She moaned louder in pain, and he forgot her skin color and tried to untangle her hair, but to no avail. The water was rushing up to her face, and she started thrashing about. The small boy had a knife on his side, which he showed her. She nodded yes to him. He then cut her beautiful hair off of the branches until she was free. She looked at him with eyes that seemed to burn through his very soul. Then she turned and dove into the water.

"When she dove in, her mighty tail broke the surface, and he could see the fish scales that covered it. They were iridescent in the light of the rising sun, and it was the most beautiful and frightening thing he had ever seen. He watched her swim away, then saw her turn around and wave goodbye. He went back to the bridge made of sticks and cut her tangled silver hair off of it. He needed proof that this really happened, if only for himself.

"What he encountered that day, he never forgot, and he never strayed from the details of this story. He was an old man when he carved her image into the staircase and her image was carved entirely from his memory. She was fierce and he was terrified of her. But, he knew he had helped save her life, and that she would not forget it or him.

"His mind was etched with what he witnessed that day. He carried the braid he had made of her silver hair in his pocket and eagerly showed it to anyone who was interested."

I was so astounded by her story of the history behind the mermaid staircase that I couldn't speak, lest I forgot one tiny detail of this story. I was at a loss for words, because I didn't know what to say after hearing that mesmerizing story. I think she realized it and proceeded to veer me toward the living room. She introduced me to her maid Rosa as she brought us coffee and banana nut bread to snack on. About that time, the heavens opened up and the rain began to pour. She had a roaring fire going in that ancient fireplace, and I felt transported to another time.

I asked her what had happened to Aoesp after he finished the staircase. She said that he lived a long and healthy life. He was never sick, ever. Being a slave, he had converted to Catholicism—the religion of his owners—and was very religious. He was also a "traiteur," or faith healer. An elderly female slave gave him the gift when he was a young man.

He was considered a very important man on the plantation, and people, both black and white, showed up at his door for him to pray for their ailments. He considered his healing abilities a gift from God and refused to accept payment in exchange for his services. The people were so grateful that they left gifts, even though he told them not to. Ms. Carine said that he lived his remaining years in a slave cabin by the cotton fields. He had received his freedom but chose to remain there with the people he had worked side by side all of his life.

"Was he allowed to get married and did he have any children?" I asked.

"Yes, the slaves in Louisiana were allowed to be married or jump the broom, as they called it," explained Ms. Carine. "He was married three times and outlived all of his wives. He had a total of twenty-two children. Ten were with his second wife and twelve with his third. As a matter of fact, Rosa is his great-great-granddaughter. She is his granddaughter by his third wife, whose name was Elsie."

As soon as the rain stopped, I got ready to leave. Ms. Carine was bobbing for apples, as the saying goes. Each time her chin drifted closer to her bosom, she'd jerk upright as though startled. I could have stayed hours longer, but she needed to rest.

As I was leaving, she asked, "Would you like to visit again?"

"I'd love to."

We made plans, to meet again the next Saturday at her home.

When I drove away, I felt like the whole visit had been a dream, surreal almost.

It was as if I had somehow stepped back in time. I wondered about the little girl in the window. She never came down, and neither Ms. Carine nor Rosa had said a word about her.

Going back to my house was stepping back into reality. I was so busy at work that I hardly had a minute to think about anything else. I worked in a law office so that meant deadlines to meet and clients to deal with. The phones rang off the hook every single minute. By the time I got off in the afternoon, I was mentally exhausted and didn't want to think about anything else. Safely back at home by the time the rain started up again, I avoided the stack of bills that'd still be there the next day and pulled out my favorite mystery novel, *Thunder Heights* by Phyllis A. Whitney. I could always count on a good book to escape reality for a little while.

Before I knew it, my work week was over and Saturday had come calling again. I called Ms. Carine to make sure our coffee date was still on. Rosa answered the telephone and assured me that Ms. Carine was indeed waiting for me to arrive.

As I drove down the winding driveway this felt different than my last visit here. As if I had been here many times before. Today, it wasn't storming and the sun was shining, but the difference was slight because the trees lining the driveway were thick and dark and cast shadows on both sides of the road.

Ms. Carine and Rosa were both sitting on the porch when I drove up.

She waved hello to me and said, "It's so nice this morning, I thought we could have our coffee outside."

"I agree," I said. Rosa went inside to retrieve hot coffee and ginger snap cookies. We sat in silence for a little while, then Ms. Carine asked me about myself. She asked if I worked outside of my home and if so, where?

I replied that I worked at a law firm, and she asked me if I enjoyed the work that I did.

When I replied, "No, I hate what I do," she looked at me thoughtfully and asked, "Have you always felt that way?"

"No, not always. When I first started, I loved it and thought it was interesting, but now I just feel stress and anxiety when I'm there."

"Yes, I can see that. You tense up just talking about it. So, let's change the subject."

I laughed and said, "Yes that's a good idea, I'd much prefer hearing about your life anyway."

Ms. Carine smiled, then sat back in her old rocker and got a far-away look in her eyes.

"I was born Carine Elizabeth Hathaway. I am the only surviving child born of Charles and Lucy Hunter Hathaway of Boston Massachusetts.

"Before I was born, my mother had already given birth to four babies, three boys stillborn and one boy who died when he turned a week old. All four of them had been given Christian names and were buried in the local cemetery.

"By the time I was born, my mother was getting on in age and she was always sick. I felt that I took care of her instead of the other way around. I was taught to clean the house at a very young age, and my father and I had to cater to her needs and wants.

"I now believe that the loss of her four children caused my mother to lose the deepest part of herself. The light in her eyes flickered out and her zest for living waned. Of course, as a child I didn't understand why my mommy was sad all of the time.

"What I do remember is how dark the house was. The blinds were always closed, and the curtains drawn. Our neighbors did try to visit with her, but she refused to see anyone. They all looked at me with pity.

"My escape was my garden. I learned how to grow a vegetable garden at a young age. There were no stores to run to and buy these things. You grew them, or you didn't eat." She laughed and said most people today couldn't imagine living like that. "What was supposed to be work turned into my greatest pleasure. I have been a gardener my entire life, and now that I'm too old to turn the dirt, I do so miss it."

I took a deep breath and decided to ask her a very personal question. "Ms. Carine, how old are you?"

She looked at me, laughed, and said, "Too old to care about how old I am! But to answer your question, I'm 99 years old."

I shook my head in disbelief and said, "I never would have guessed."

"I guess now you're going to ask yourself why you're spending your time with such an old lady."

"Oh no, not at all," I said. "It makes you more interesting to me. You have lived through so many changes in our world and I for one want to know all about it. Please, keep going with your story."

"Like I said, things were pretty dreary inside, so I spent most of my days outside. I had been taught to grow vegetables for us to eat, and once I had that under control, I started planting flowers. I dug up wild flowers wherever I found some and replanted them in my garden.

"Our neighbor, Mrs. Kathleen Carrier, who lived down the road saw what I was doing and started giving me cuttings from her garden. She was nice to me and explained how different plants needed to be planted in different areas of the yard. She had a very beautiful garden so I trusted what she was telling me was correct. She was a little put off that my own mother was not doing this and said so. I tried to explain to her that my mother was sick.

"She said, 'Maybe if she would get out of that dark closed-up house and into the sunlight, she might feel better. She may realize she's not the only person in this world who has suffered a loss. She may understand that yes, she lost four children, but then she was blessed with a daughter who survived. She has a daughter who lives and breathes and needs her mother.'

"I felt uncomfortable with her saying those things about my mother, even if they were true. As much as I didn't want to admit it, I agreed with her. Many times, I wanted to tell my mother the same things. Just get out of bed and let some sunlight into this house. Every day, I cut fresh flowers for the house and always put some in her room, but she never noticed. If she did notice, she never said a word. That was her way, to take everything given to her and give nothing back."

"Where was your father in all of this?" I asked her.

"Father was never around," she said. "He worked at a newspaper company where he was in charge of printing the paper. After work, he went out with his co-workers to drink at the local bar. He pretty much left mother in my care."

"You must have been so terribly lonely," I said to her.

Ms. Carine looked at me and said, "My dear, you cannot imagine how alone I was. I think what kept me sane was that I was so busy working. But I was young and yearned for things I didn't have, like friends and fun."

"What about boyfriends?" I asked. "I know you were beautiful because you still are. You must have had some boys interested in you."

"Yes, there were a few boys curious about me, but I was not attracted to any of them. Most of them thought of me as strange. I went to school then went straight home to do my chores. I didn't socialize with them. I didn't have time. My childhood was not a normal childhood, but then I didn't know what normal was, did I?

"Anyway, I got through it and managed to also graduate from high school. I then took on a part-time job ironing clothes for a wealthy family in our town. The lady of the house was called Nadine Steller. She was kind and paid me well. She knew my background and felt that I had managed to raise myself quite well in spite of my circumstances. She knew I had a beautiful garden and enlisted me to teach her yardman how to grow roses like mine. When I did, she rewarded me with money and her friendship.

"She was older than my mother, and she was the first real friend I ever had. She was an avid traveler and shared everything she had seen and learned with me. She taught me how to be a lady and how to dress. She was trying to help me to learn how to interact with others. I started spending more and more time with her and away from home. She always had company stopping by, so I was meeting new people. I didn't feel comfortable around them, but they ignored me most of the time. That was fine with me, because I didn't much like any of them anyway.

"Nadine was planning her annual holiday party one year and she invited me. I had never been to a party, so I was most anxious about it. I made every kind of excuse about why I couldn't be there. 'First and foremost,' I told her, 'I don't have anything to wear, and I don't have any dancing shoes.' Those were two absolutely good reasons not to attend. But deep down in my heart, I really wanted to go."

Rosa came in, interrupting her tale. "It's getting late. Ms. Carine, you need to take your pills."

I stood up quickly and apologized for staying so late. I promised her that I would be back next week for what was turning into a weekly ritual between us. As I was walking away, I turned and saw Rosa helping Ms. Carine into the house. I nodded goodbye to Rosa, and she just stared at me. I hadn't yet figured her out.

As I was driving away, I swore I saw a little girl hiding behind a tree on the side of the driveway. I stopped my car, left it running, and stepped out of the car into the woods.

"Hello, is anyone there?" I asked. I didn't see anyone, so I got back into my car, but I could feel someone staring at me. It was a very uneasy feeling, and I drove away wondering who this child belonged to.

Work was hectic as usual and my week flew by. Some of my friends invited me to go shopping with them on Saturday, but I hesitated because I would have to cancel my visit with Ms. Carine. They didn't understand what was going on with me and this lady I had just met. I was having a hard time explaining it to them when I didn't fully understand it myself. Instead of arguing with my friends, I canceled my visit with Ms. Carine and spent the day with them. I found myself bored by their talk and regretted canceling my visit.

I wanted to hear more about her life. I wanted to know if she had attended the party she had been invited to, and I really wanted to ask her about the little girl hanging around her house.

I called Ms. Carine when I got home and asked if I could come and visit the next day. She sounded a bit miffed but said yes, I could come in the afternoon. When I got there, Rosa let me in and said that Ms. Carine would be with me in a minute. It gave me a chance to walk around and look at her house.

I asked Rosa if she had a hard time cleaning this house, which was very large.

She stared at me with a funny look on her face and said, "No, not at all. Why would you think that?" she asked.

I said, "Well, just the first floor is a lot to clean, but you've got the upstairs as well."

"No one ever goes upstairs." She wouldn't quite meet my eyes, focusing instead on polishing the already gleaming banister.

"Not even to clean?"

"No one is allowed upstairs."

I'd been looking forward to seeing the whole house, not just part of it. A shame I wouldn't be able to. Maybe one day.

Rosa looked annoyed with me so I left that subject alone, but I thought that whole conversation was strange. Ms. Carine had not yet made her entrance, and I was feeling a bit uneasy. When I'm nervous, I can't stop talking. It's a bad habit, but one I can't help.

So, I kept rambling. "Rosa, do you have a little granddaughter?"

"No, I don't have any children. Why do you ask?"

I told her that I thought I had seen a little girl from the upstairs window the very first time I had visited here.

She looked visibly shaken and said, "Well, you are mistaken. There are no children here and certainly not upstairs."

As Ms. Carine walked in she looked at Rosa and asked her if everything was alright in here.

Rosa responded and said, "Yes, I was just going into the kitchen to prepare the coffee for you and Ms. Danielle."

Ms. Carine looked suspiciously at Rosa and said, "The wind has picked up and it's getting cooler. Please add some wood to the fire so we can continue our story."

For a few minutes, she and I sat and rocked before the fire, each of us lost in our own thoughts.

Very quietly, Ms. Carine began telling her story right where she had left off.

"There were a hundred reasons why I shouldn't have gone to Nadine's party. But I did go. I was amazed at the beautiful dresses worn by all the girls. I hardly recognized some of them with their faces made up and their hair piled high on their heads. They looked beautiful and I just felt out of place and insecure. Nadine had picked out my dress and shoes and even though she had good intentions, the dress was too big and the color was wrong. I stood in a corner and tried to disappear.

"No one paid any attention to me so I was able to stand back from the crowd and watch them. Being on the outside looking in was nothing new to me. I was very good at figuring people out, I had years of experience in that area, but I was hoping that at least one person would surprise me tonight. None did. They all acted the way I knew they would. Haughty, arrogant little biddies they were. I haven't yet told you why they all treated me the way they did. There was talk since the time I was born that my mother had stepped out on my father. Do you know what that means?"

I nodded yes.

"Talk around town was that my mother thought my father's seed was cursed, on account of her losing their four babies. There was talk that she went to fortune tellers and gypsies, trying to communicate with the dead. Her own mother had killed herself when my mother was only sixteen, and she never got over losing her.

"She wanted to know why her mother had taken her own life, and why she herself had lost four babies. She wanted answers, and so she reached out to these people to help her.

"There was one man, a gypsy, who was seen going into our home when father was at work. He went there supposedly for a séance. They said he was a striking man with golden hair and eyes the color of emeralds. A man no woman would forget. Well, nine months later, I was born. My hair was the color of the sun and my eyes were a clear light green. Spooky eyes, some would say.

"My mother and father both had dark brown hair with dark eyes. I never fit in from the start, and my father always doubted that I was his. He didn't necessarily treat me badly, he just ignored me. It was as if I didn't exist. She laughed a bitter laugh and said, "Hell, sometimes I even wondered myself if I existed.

"As far as the people in our town were concerned, my mother was an adulteress and I a bastard child. I think that was why she never went out of the house. She knew what they thought of her, and nothing she could say or do would convince them otherwise. She must have been terribly lonely, but instead of loving and spoiling me, she blamed me for her circumstances. Anyway, I'm getting a little off track, so let's get back to the night of the dance.

"There was this one man at the dance whom I had never laid eyes on before. Apparently, none of the women there had either, because all eyes were on him. He was tall, dark, and handsome, and our eyes locked from across the room.

"Nadine showed him around the room and introduced him to everyone there. Finally, they made their way to me. I can't lie, his wavy black hair fascinated me. Why, it almost touched his collar! He had the most penetrating black eyes. They seemed to look right through me. But it was his accent that most intrigued me. I couldn't place it. I thought maybe it was French, but I couldn't be sure.

"The one thing I could be sure of was that he seemed interested in me. No matter who he was talking to, he kept his eyes on me. After what seemed like an eternity, he made his way around the room and back to me. His name was Joshua Dubois, and he was from Louisiana. He said he was a Cajun Frenchman from the great state of Louisiana, and he seemed quite proud of it, I must say. He was there on business for his father and he would be in town for just one week.

"He wanted to know if I was available tomorrow to take him on a tour of our city. He apologized for being so forward, but he said that time was of the essence. My heart was racing in my chest, I could hardly breathe. Of all the girls at the party, he had chosen me. I informed him that I had a job and worked daily.

"He said, 'All right, what time will you be done?'

"I said, 'Four o'clock, at the earliest.'

"Joshua replied, 'Good, I will come by to pick you up at five.'

"I was so surprised, I just nodded in agreement.

"Well, pick me up he did, and it was glorious. He took me to the finest restaurant in town. We walked everywhere while I pointed out all of the town's businesses and where everyone lived. He made me feel so special, and I was smitten with him.

"I didn't even mind that I was the center of attention and that everywhere we went, people were staring at us. Every day for a week, it was the same routine, I worked then waited for him to come and pick me up.

"He never asked to meet my parents, which I thought very odd. When I mentioned that my mother was complaining about how much time I was spending away from home, he just looked at me and said, 'How would you like to come to Louisiana with me?'

I wasn't sure what he meant. He saw the confusion on my face, and he heard the silence of my thoughts.

"I said, 'I'm not sure what you're asking me.'

"He laughed and said, 'I am offering you a new life away from here, a life where you will be taken care of, where you will have servants who will do the work for you.'

"I replied, 'What are your intentions toward me?

"He said, 'I want to make you my wife. I find you quite fascinating and, most important, I really like you. Liking someone is more important than loving them, don't you think? You can love someone and not like them, but that makes for a miserable existence. It is much easier to live with someone that you like. Love will come in time.'

"'But we have only known each other for a week, what will people think?' I asked.

"'Do you really care what these people think of you?' he asked. 'You have not been treated well by these people about whom you are concerned. You have not been treated well by your own parents, from what I've been told. You will never have to see them again. All

I ask is that you think about my offer. I leave to go home day after tomorrow.'

"He dropped me off at home, and I told him that I would consider his offer. My mother was furious when she saw me and let me know how behind I was on all of my chores. I told her that I would stay home the next day and catch up on the housework and the gardening. *It would give me time to think about my choices.* All I could do was think about Joshua and his somewhat awkward proposal of marriage.

"I hardly slept at all that night, as I was torn between my home and this man. I was very attracted to him, but at the same time, I realized that I didn't know him at all. I thought about the possibility of never seeing my parents again, and then I thought about never seeing Joshua again. I was so confused."

At that point of her story, Ms. Carine looked at me with such sadness in her eyes that I couldn't help but feel sorry for her.

Suddenly, I felt a chill run through my body and I shivered. The fire had gone out, and the sun was going down.

Ms. Carine shook her head as if she was having a hard time coming back to this time and place.

She said, "My dear, I believe I've kept you far too long."

I said, "No not at all, I have enjoyed every minute of it, but I must hurry and get home."

I gathered my purse, told her goodbye, and left, promising to come back next Saturday.

I stepped off of her porch and felt someone watching me. I turned and looked toward what I still thought was a graveyard and saw the little girl standing behind the gate. I waved to her, but she only stared at me. The wind picked up, and the leaves from the huge old pecan trees started falling. I looked back one more time, but she was gone. I quickly got into my car. I suddenly wanted to get out of here and just go home.

I 'd told my co-worker Justine about my visits with Ms. Carine and had shared a little of her story. She was as mystified as I was. She was especially interested in the little girl I kept seeing.

She said, "You need to ask Ms. Carine who this child belongs to. If she has lived in this house all of her adult life, she would have to know who her neighbors are. How much land does she have with this house?"

I said, "I don't know. Why?"

She said, "Well, it makes a difference with how close her nearest neighbor is to her. A child that young wouldn't travel very far by herself."

That made sense. So I made up my mind to ask Ms. Carine a few more personal questions.

When I went to bed that Friday night, I tossed and turned for hours, unable to sleep. I kept thinking about everything Justine and I had speculated on, and all of the questions running through my mind that I wanted to ask Ms. Carine. Was that a graveyard toward the back of her property? If so, who was buried there? Who was the little girl I kept seeing, and why did Rosa get upset when I asked about her? For some reason, when I was with Ms. Carine, I never thought to ask her any of these questions. I always felt transported to another place and time when I was in her presence. The only way to explain how it feels when I am with her is that time stands still.

I awoke tired and grumpy from a lack of sleep. When I finally did fall asleep, I dreamt I was at Ms. Carine's house, walking along the brick pathway to the back of her yard. In the distance, I could see the wrought iron fence but couldn't make out what it was surrounding.

I wasn't sure if a garden or a graveyard lay beyond that fence. I could make out rose bushes inside of the fenced area that were overgrown and unkempt. I kept walking slowly toward the area when suddenly that same little girl appeared to my left. She was pointing towards the gate, staring at it. I woke up with a start.

I was very anxious to meet with Ms. Carine that day. I made up my mind that I was going to get some of my questions answered. I wanted to see more of her house. I had only been in the entrance with the staircase and the living room. It was a big house and I was determined to explore it. That Saturday, I decided to treat Ms. Carine, so I made a bread pudding to bring with me. I didn't want to take advantage of her hospitality, after all.

The sky was full of fat gray clouds and it was drizzling when I left my house. The wind was picking up and the temperature was dropping fast. A cold front was expected later today but it looked like it was coming in early. The one thing that is certain in Louisiana is that the weather changes constantly. Smoke drifted out of the stately manor's chimney, and I couldn't wait to sit before that roaring fire.

Ms. Carine met me at the door and she was delighted with my gift of bread pudding. She had Rosa fix us each a steaming mug of hot chocolate. She walked with a noticeable stoop in her shoulders that day.

I asked her if she was feeling okay and she smiled and said, "It's the cold, makes my joints hurt something bad. It's why I had central heating put in a few years ago. Danielle, I know you love old houses but they are awful drafty and cold in the winter time."

"Did you have new insulation put in too?" I asked.

"No, I didn't. You know this house was insulated with bousillage when it was built. That means that they used a mixture of clay and Spanish moss to seal the gaps between the boards of the house. That is still the only insulation it has. The only thing I changed was adding central heating about thirty years ago and the addition of another bathroom upstairs. As big as this house is, it only had one bathroom downstairs. When I moved here with my husband, our bedroom was upstairs. It was difficult sharing a bathroom with his whole family. I put up with it for a few years and eventually talked him into adding one in our bedroom. Our bedroom was so large that there was plenty of room for the addition. It was the only time that I requested changing anything in this house."

Rosa came in with our hot chocolate and the pudding I had prepared.

Ms. Carine said, "We'll eat and drink, then take a quick tour of the house. Before I get started on my story, I want to get to know you a little better. Tell me, Danielle, what is your passion in life? What do you love to do?"

I sipped my hot chocolate while I thought about what it was I really wanted to do. "I love a good book, and I've always wanted to write one."

"Why haven't you?" She set her cup down to take a bite of pudding.

"I don't know where to start." I'd always thought of writing a book, but never about the actual process of writing.

"I think you just have to write something down, anything." She smiled her knowing smile again.

"My problem is that I work all day and put all of my mental energy into my job. The stories come to me when I lay my head down to sleep. I can't get up to write them down because I need my rest for another day. When I do have time to rest, I can't think of anything to write about. In other words, I don't have a story."

Ms. Carine thought about that for a minute. "I don't believe you have to have a story to begin writing, only an idea. Next time you have an idea, just jot it down. Maybe it will turn into a story, maybe not. But what will it hurt to write it down?"

"That makes sense to me. The next time I have an idea, I'll do that."

"What else are you interested in?" she asked.

"I love photography. I have always been intrigued by pictures, especially of people. I am a part-time photographer. I got into it as a hobby and occasionally make a little money with it. When I was a child, I was fascinated with my mother's photo albums.

"I looked at them throughout my childhood and always tried to figure out the mood of the person in the photo. I still love to look at pictures, especially the old ones," I replied.

"That tells me that you have a sensitive and artistic personality," said Ms. Carine.

"I guess that's true, because I've always been told that I'm very sensitive." When she paused to sip more hot chocolate, I took the opportunity to request something that, for whatever reason, I'd been dreading. Worst case scenario, she'd say no. But I had to ask. "Ms. Carine, I would love a tour of your house when your arthritis isn't bothering you."

"I will show you around the downstairs. It actually helps my arthritis when I move around some," she replied.

"Okay, if you're sure, I would love to see it," I said.

"We will start the tour here in the room you are most familiar with," replied Ms. Carine. "This is the informal living room and library. Pull one of those curtains aside."

When I moved the heavy velour drapes, I noticed the size of the windows for the first time. Each window stood nearly as tall as the walls themselves.

Ms. Carine smiled. "When the weather's nice, we open the drapes and flood the room with natural light."

The drapes also hid bookshelves even taller than the windows. "I don't remember seeing a library in here. How in the world did I not notice that? Your bookshelves go all the way up to the ceiling." Hundreds of old books filled the shelves. It was a collection to treasure by anyone's standard. "How could I have missed that?"

She chuckled. "Don't let that worry you. This room is always very dark, and the library is hidden in the shadows, is all. I can assure you it has been here since the house was built."

But it did bother me. I had been in this room several times and never noticed the books. Impossible, I love books. I am drawn to them. *How could I miss a bookcase that filled a wall?*

We walked out of the library and into the entrance with the amazing staircase. To the right of the staircase, a door led to a beautiful sitting room.

"This is the formal living room," stated Ms. Carine.

A beautiful grand piano took up one corner of the room with a gorgeous fireplace on the side of it. A huge painting of a young woman hung above the fireplace.

This woman stood in front of the very same fireplace with her arms folded while she leaned against the mantel. She was wearing an exquisite royal blue velvet, floor-length gown. Her long blonde hair hung loosely down her back in cascading curls. Hair from both sides of her head had been pulled back with an elaborate ivory comb. But the look on her face is what held my attention. It made me want to cry. A look of such heartbreaking sadness, I couldn't help but being moved.

I looked at Ms. Carine and said, "Is this you?"

She nodded and lowered her eyes.

"It's a beautiful portrait of you and I feel moved just viewing it. You just seem so heartbroken. Were you?"

"Yes," Ms. Carine replied. "When I posed for this portrait, I was at one of the lowest points in my life. It was not my idea to pose for this painting. My husband insisted that I do it. It has always hung here and it is the main reason I keep this room closed."

She then proceeded to leave the room, so I followed her out. The next door opened up to the bathroom. It was a medium size room, but it was small compared to the other rooms. A big, free-standing claw foot bathtub was the crowning point of the room. The walls were a sickly pale green and the ceiling was so high that it felt off-balance. For some reason, I felt uncomfortable in this room and was relieved when we walked out.

Behind the next door lay the only bedroom downstairs; Ms. Carine's room. A huge, four poster bed dominated the space, but left plenty of room to maneuver around the large bedroom. Two beautiful, stained glass windows opened up to the outside and looked out over the orchard. Pillows lined a long window seat, offering a place for the room's occupants to lounge on. I could imagine myself laying there with a good book, listening to the rain softly falling. I told Ms. Carine that she had a beautiful bedroom and she just smiled. I could have lingered longer, but we moved on to the next room. The formal dining area was an enormous room which held a cypress table that sat twelve people. A beautiful antique buffet was placed against the wall with a giant gilded mirror hanging above it.

Two old world, gorgeous, glass chandeliers hung over the table. Ms. Carine told me that this room was once used to hold formal dances, and so was always the prettiest room in the house.

Just beyond the dining room, the kitchen resided at the back of the house, the layout typical of these old homes. With no air conditioning back in those days, the kitchen was usually hot from cooking. Therefore, the back doors were typically left open to help cool the space and draw the heat away from the home's interior.

This kitchen was amazing. The cabinets were original to the house. They rose up so high that a ladder was needed to reach into the upper shelves.

Several of the cabinet doors were made of lead cut glass that displayed the gorgeous crystal glassware stacked within. A breakfast nook—surrounded by windows overlooking a small back porch—sat nestled in the back of the kitchen, with a butler's pantry on the side.

Ms. Carine was getting tired and suggested that we head back to the library for another cup of hot chocolate. I really wanted to explore a little more of the house, but I was happy with what I did get to see. And I was eager to get back to her story.

"Where did I leave off last time we met?"

"You were trying to make a choice between staying with your parents or moving away with Joshua. I know what choice you made because you married him and moved here, but I'd still like to hear the story."

Ms. Carine smiled at me. "The one thing I have learned throughout my life is that we should never assume anything, because when we do, we are usually wrong.

"I tried to convince myself to leave my home for this man that I had only known for a week. But in the end, fear of the unknown had a greater impact on my decision.

Joshua arrived at my home the morning of his departure. He

informed my parents of his intentions toward me. They looked at me in astonishment, horrified that I would even consider his proposal.

"Joshua never asked me what choice I had made. He just assumed that I had chosen to go with him. After he informed my parents of our plans, he asked me if I had my things ready. All of this time, my mother and father never uttered a word. They just sat there with their heads hanging down.

"Up until that moment, I had not made a choice. I made my decision then.

"'No, Joshua. As much as my heart is breaking, I cannot leave with you. I have only known you for one week. My mother is sick and without help. I need time to get to know you and time to make sure that my parents can cope when I am gone. If you want me as your wife, you will honor my request.'

"Joshua looked at me in disbelief. I don't think it had occurred to him that my answer could be no. He just shook his head and stared at the floor.

"He said, 'I will be leaving for Louisiana in two hours. If you come to your senses and change your mind, you know where to find me.'

"I watched the man of my dreams walk out of my house and out of my life. All of my blood rushed to my head, and I felt like I was going to pass out. I felt like I'd made the wrong choice.

"My mother looked at me and said, 'It's about time you use your head. Good for nothing trash from Louisiana. What man proposes marriage after only one week? And he's a Cajun. He probably lives in a shack in the swamps. You have obligations here. I'm sick, too sick to clean this house and work the garden. Your responsibility is to me, not him.'

"I looked at her in horror and ran out of the room crying. I flung myself on my bed and cried my heart out. There was still a chance. I thought of packing my bags and going to meet him. But as attracted to him as I was, I still was not sure who this man really was.

I needed time, and he wasn't giving it to me. Why was my life so difficult and why was it so hard for me to make a decision? I felt so alone with no one to confide in. Then I got angry at Joshua for pushing me to make a decision that I was not yet ready to make. I decided to go and confront him before he left for his home.

"When I arrived at Ms. Nadine's house, she let me in with a question in her eyes.

"I told her that I needed to speak with Joshua for a minute.

"She nodded and walked out to get him. My stomach was in knots from the stress I was under. I took a deep breath and closed my eyes. When I opened them, he was standing there staring at me.

"I said, 'I need to speak with you.'

"He replied, 'I also need to speak to you.'

"'I don't know how you do things in the south, but here we show our parents respect.'

"Joshua shook his head and said, 'Yes, I was also raised to respect my parents and my elders.'

"'If what you say is true, I couldn't tell by the way you treated my parents. You told them you were marrying their daughter instead of asking for their permission.'

"Joshua started to interrupt me, but I held my hand up to stop him.

"'You never asked me what my answer was. You just assumed it was yes. Is that how I'll be treated in the future?'

"Joshua looked at me with surprise and a bit of humor.

"'If you marry me, I promise to always treat you and your family with respect. I will contact my father by telegram and advise him of my intention to stay in Boston another month. That should give us time to get to know one another and time for your parents to adjust.

It will also give you time to find someone to take care of your ailing mother if, in fact, your answer is yes.'

"What he said made me very happy and relieved. My stomach suddenly relaxed and my stress was gone. That's all it was, I told myself, I just needed Joshua to give me time." With that statement, Ms. Carine gave a big sigh and put her head against the chair she was sitting in.

I excused myself to go to the bathroom.

"Of course, dear, you know where it is. Make yourself at home."

If I could have held it until I got home, I would have. That bathroom gave me the creeps. But I told myself that I was just being silly. There was a chill in that room, and I found myself shivering. I hurried up and did my business and found myself ready to go home. When I stepped out of the bathroom, I thought I heard footsteps on the stairs. I found myself going up the stairs even though I knew I shouldn't.

When I reached the fourth stair, Rosa walked into the foyer and said, "What are you doing?"

I jumped when she spoke and said, "I thought I heard footsteps on the stairs."

She raised her eyebrows and replied, "I already told you no one goes upstairs. The footsteps you heard were mine."

I walked down the stairs with her watching me the whole way down. I went in to tell Ms. Carine I was leaving, but the poor old woman was asleep in her chair.

Rosa said to me, "You two had a long visit today, it wore her out. I'll tell her you said goodbye."

It was already dark and cold when I walked out of the house. The moon had risen in the sky, and the light from it shone on the fence and on the pond at the back of the property.

It was a beautiful view, so I pulled out my trusty Kodak and snapped a quick photo of it. When I got into my car, I looked back at the house and saw Rosa watching me from the window.

When I went back to work on Monday, Justine wanted details of my visit. She was upset with me for neglecting to ask Ms. Carine about the little girl. To appease her, I informed her that I had finally gotten a tour of the house, at least of the downstairs. She made me promise to try and take some pictures of the house the next time I visited. Then I remembered the picture I had taken with my camera last night while leaving. I hurried to the pharmacy and dropped off my film to get it developed. Later that afternoon, I picked my pictures up. I rushed back to the office to show Justine my prints. The picture was both beautiful and creepy at the same time. I showed it to Justine, and she stared at it in awe. She said there was no way in hell that she would ever be caught there after dark.

I looked closer at the fence and could barely make out a small figure of a child sitting with her back against the fence. Justine looked at it, and she said she didn't see anyone. I was sure it was the little girl, but I knew I could be wrong because it was really cold last night and late when I left. It was much too late for a small child to be out, and alone in that weather.

The first thing I did when I got home was look for my magnifying glass. I zoomed in on the fence and could see vines growing around the old posts wrapping themselves around each of the wrought iron spindles.

I could barely make out what looked like a small shoulder of a child perched against the fence. My curiosity was piqued. Who was this little girl, who did she belong to, and why was I the only one seeing this child?

The next day at work I did a loan closing for an older gentleman named Stan Broussard. Being an older gentleman, he wanted to know if I was from here and who my family was. These questions he asked me were some that I had grown accustomed to.

Living in a small town people always try to place you with someone that they know. He said he was familiar with the area where I lived. I decided to ask him if he knew Ms. Carine or at least knew of the old home place. He remembered hearing his parents speak of that family. He said that they were wealthy and once owned the largest cotton plantation in the state. He remembered that there was a lot of tragedy associated with their family. As far as he knew, he thought that they had all passed away a long time ago and the old house had been abandoned or torn down.

I told him that Ms. Carine was very much alive and still living in that very house. He shook his head with a look of confusion.

He said, "That just can't be, she would be very, very old."

I laughed and said, "Well she is old, but very much alive. I have been visiting with her every week for a couple of months now."

I knew from the look on his face that he thought that I must be talking about someone else. That conversation bothered me because here was someone who remembered Ms. Carine's family, but he was sure they were all long gone. He was old himself and said he was a child when his parents spoke of her family. I won't lie; I was very confused at this point. I decided that I would tell Ms. Carine about my conversation with him.

A message had been left taped to my front door from Ms. Carine, apologizing for falling asleep on me. She asked that I come earlier tomorrow so that we would have more time to visit. We were in the dead of winter now, and the days were shorter. I called to let her know that I would be there, and she said that Rosa would prepare a lunch for us.

———————

I woke up to temperatures in the low forties, with warnings of a hard freeze that night. I wanted to call and cancel the visit but my curiosity got the best of me. I'd have to make sure to leave her house early today because by nightfall, there could be ice on the roads.

The winding driveway to her house was especially desolate today. The giant trees were bare and the sky above them was a dark, menacing gray. Gusts of wind picked up the dead brown leaves and swirled them up into the air. When I made my way around the curve of the driveway, I got a surreal feeling just looking at the house. The wood was aged and graying, fitting perfectly into the bleak landscape. You could live in this area all your life and never know that this house was here. I'm sure in the summertime, with flowers blooming and the grass green, it would be beautiful. But right now, it looked abandoned and dead.

It felt like a memory out of the past, almost like stepping back in time. I had to mentally shake myself out of this feeling of dread. I always enjoyed Ms. Carine's stories, but lately I left there with more questions than answers. Still, she was a gracious host. I needed to compose myself.

Rosa made a beef and corn soup; perfect for this weather. She also had homemade bread baking in the oven. I felt better already. Ms. Carine's eyes brightened as I approached, and she animatedly waved me over to take a seat. I decided to bring up the conversation I had with the elderly gentleman a few days ago. Ms. Carine didn't recognize his name or his family. She said he must have been thinking of another family, not hers.

She quickly changed the subject. I took the hint and let it go. The wind was blowing so hard that it sounded like an animal wailing just outside the windows.

Maybe the weather was to blame for the unease settling within me. She glanced at the fire, and then began her tale anew. I didn't have to remind her where she left off. She went right into her story.

"Joshua had received a telegram from his father and gotten his permission to stay another month. He never told me the reason he gave his father. I just assumed he told him the truth, that he met someone he wanted to marry and needed time with her and her family. He was everything I dreamt of. He made me feel special and surprised me with little gifts. He gave my mother attention and brought her flowers. He brought whiskey for my father and listened to his stories. I saw my parents in a totally new light when he was around. He enlisted Ms. Nadine's help in finding a dependable and affordable woman to come in and help my mother with the daily chores.

"Somehow, he completely won over my family, and now they were pushing me to hurry and marry this wonderful, rich young man. When I think back on it, he never spoke to me of his family or his life in Louisiana. The only time I could get a glimpse of it was when he was sharing tales with my mother and father. My parents and Joshua made plans. We would be married before the end of the month. It just wouldn't be right for a young girl of nineteen to leave with him unless we were married first.

"That month was a frenzy of excitement. I didn't have a minute to think. I did ask him if his parents would be upset that they couldn't attend their son's wedding. He replied that we would plan a celebration with their family and friends when we arrived in Louisiana.

"We were married in the church I had gone to all my life. My father never went to church as he saw no use for it, and my mother had given up on religion with the loss of her first child. But when I was old enough, I went alone. I loved the peace and solitude of the church.

I had many conversations with the Lord there. I could always talk to him about the burdens I carried. I knew that he was always listening. It was important to me that I be married there.

"Although I spent my life feeling left out and judged by the children I grew up with, it seemed that now, they all wanted to be my friends.

"No man is an island and no matter what anyone may claim, no one chooses to be alone. Sometimes, it's just the way life is. So, I accepted their attempts at friendship and enjoyed it for this brief period of time.

"A wedding was always a cause for celebration, and this one was no different. We had food, drink and music. Ms. Nadine pulled her wedding gown out of storage and altered it for me.

"It was a beautiful floor length gown, with cream colored lace. There were pearl buttons on the sleeves and along the neckline. The veil covered my face and was so long, it fell to the floor. For the first time in my life, I felt and looked like a princess.

"Joshua spared no expense on the food and drink. He left my father with enough money to last them for a year. The wedding celebration was over as quickly as it had begun. Joshua rented the nicest room in the little hotel where the celebration was held. He was very sociable and friendly with everyone there, except me. I felt like we had no connection between us at all.

"I figured that since the party was for us, he was just being gracious. He must have been trying to make a good impression on everyone there. That had to be the reason. I tried not to worry about the lack of attraction between us.

"I was very nervous about my wedding night, as every girl is for her first time. But he'd had too much to drink, and he actually passed out fully-clothed on the bed. I removed his shoes and cried myself to sleep.

"We left for Louisiana the following morning."

CHAPTER TWO

LOUISIANA BOUND

"It took approximately one month to make the trip from Boston to Louisiana. We traveled from Boston to New York City by horse and carriage. It was a long and tedious trip. We took the train from New York to New Orleans. From New Orleans to Joshua's home, we again traveled by carriage.

"I tried to make conversation with him but it was as though he didn't even hear me. He shut me out. He said he was tired and asked me to just be silent for a while. That was something I knew how to do, only too well. But this was different. I had never traveled anywhere and the countryside seemed to go on forever. The small glimpse of city life that I saw intrigued me. We spent one night at a hotel in New York City. It was heavenly to finally have a bath and sleep in a real bed.

"I was beginning to wonder if this man I had married was devoid of any passion. We still had not consummated our marriage. The closest he had come so far was to occasionally squeeze my hand. "

With the thought of that memory, Ms. Carine laughed.

"But that one night in the hotel changed that. I was attracted to Joshua, and I believed that he was attracted to me. Our lovemaking was clumsy and strained and was over as soon as it began. So much for the fairytale in my mind of what romance should be. That night, the reality of what I had got myself into, began to set in. Still, I tried to convince myself that maybe we were exhausted from traveling. Time would tell.

"The day had finally arrived and Joshua advised me that we were only an hour away from his home. I had never seen him so excited and talkative. He was like a different person altogether. I, on the other hand, had a case of butterflies in my stomach.

"What if they didn't like me? What if I didn't like them? He'd told me so little of them, I wasn't sure what to expect. All I knew was that they owned a cotton plantation, the biggest one in the state. He and his father ran the plantation, and his mother ruled over the household and the servants. He had an older brother named Robert who wasn't quite right in the head and a younger sister named Stella that he doted on.

"Now, understand, he revealed these facts to me when we were an hour from his home. Until then, I was unaware that he had a sister and a brother.

"I asked him then, 'Do you think your mother and father will approve of me? Do you think your sister and I can become friends?'"

"He looked at me oddly and quietly said, 'I haven't told them about you yet.'"

"I was shocked, how could that be?

"'Didn't you ask your father for permission to stay and court me?'

"'No,' he replied. 'I told him I had further business to attend to. Besides, I don't need permission to get married. I am a grown man of twenty-nine years and know my own mind.'

"That statement took me by surprise. I knew he was older than me, but not by ten years. That reminded me of how little I knew about this man I'd married. Why would he hide our wedding from his family? I thought I was going to his home for a celebration, and now I was finding out that they knew nothing about me. As far as I was concerned, he had already broken the bonds of trust between us."

At that moment, Rosa came into the library and announced that it was noon and lunch was ready. We made our way into the kitchen and sat at the breakfast table. The breakfast nook was surrounded by windows, and we enjoyed a view of the backyard. I could make out part of the fence where I had seen the little girl.

I took a deep breath and said, "Ms. Carine, does the old fence enclose a garden or a graveyard?"

She looked at me with a frown on her face and I saw her eyes flash with anger.

She sighed deeply and said, "If you must know, it is our family cemetery."

I apologized to her for being nosy. She gave a big sigh and looked out the window toward the fence. Since she was already displeased with me, I went ahead and asked her about the little girl.

"Ms. Carine, you may think this odd, but I was wondering if you know who the little girl is that I keep seeing on your property?"

Her face paled and she grabbed the table to keep her hands from shaking. She said, "This is the first I hear of a little girl trespassing on my property."

Rosa had been standing still during this conversation, but she now turned and looked at us. She said, "Ms. Danielle mentioned that she thought she had seen a child upstairs the first time she visited. I assured her that there were no children here and certainly not in the house."

"Well, that would be correct," said Ms. Carine. "I will have Rosa inform the closest neighbor that a young child has been seen wondering about my property."

I felt better finally telling her about the girl but still had no idea who she was. I decided to change the subject and ask about the slaves and how they lived their lives. "Ms. Carine, you told me that most of the slaves converted to Catholicism. Did I understand that correctly?"

"Yes," she said. "Most of the slaves did convert. But there were still many that practiced the religion of voodoo. Most of them were uneducated, and all of them were very superstitious. In fact, almost everyone at that time was superstitious in one way or another."

"The plantation had acquired a female slave named Diedre who practiced the art of voodoo or, as some people call it, black magic. The master of the plantation where she lived suddenly died. All of his slaves were sold. Diedre was old, ugly and not worth buying. Her owners got rid of her by saying that she could make her own medicine and that she had healing powers. She was feared by everyone on this plantation because of her curses and potions. There were rumors that she poisoned her master, but no one knew for sure. The one thing they did know was that bad things started to happen at all of the surrounding farms, and because they were superstitious, they assumed it was her fault. The owner of the plantation that had acquired her and the owners of the surrounding farms got together and made a plan to be rid of her. But no one wanted to be responsible for doing it. They were afraid she would put a curse on them or their families."

"What happened to her?" I asked.

"They decided to give Deidre her freedom, as long as she left the plantation and did not return," said Ms. Carine.

"So, she just left?" I asked.

"No, it didn't happen quite that easily," replied Ms. Carine. "That Diedre was a smart one. She agreed to leave if they let her live in an old shack at the back of the swamp. They also had to send their carpenters to repair the old shack for her to live in. It could only be reached by a *pirogue*. She promised if they did what she asked, she would never leave that shack. She also promised she would never return to the plantation.

So, every day for a week, her master sent his carpenters to the shack to repair the old tin roof and floors that had rotted away. Those men were frightened to death of her but they had no choice in the matter. Aoesp was a young man then and had already been given the gift of healing. She saw him as an equal because of his healing powers, and she didn't try to use her black magic to frighten him. He wasn't afraid of her. He thought she was doing only what was needed to survive.

"Because he had no fear of her black magic, he was chosen to deliver her to the shack in the swamps and to leave her there forever. Foolishly, the plantation owners believed she would perish there with no way to leave the shack. They underestimated Diedre and her will to live.

"Every time a person showed up at her shack needing a cure or a potion, they brought her food, clothes, or whiskey. She used these people and their supplies to help herself survive in the swamps.

"They never once thought about how many desperate people would seek out Diedre for her cures and love potions, or how many women would risk their lives getting lost in the swamp to find her. She had the medicine they needed to rid their bellies of their unwanted pregnancies. Many of these women were lost in the swamp and never made it back home."

"What ended up happening to her?" I asked.

"I don't really know," said Ms. Carine.

"It looks like I wasted all of our time asking you about the slaves instead of finding out what happened when you and Joshua arrived at his home."

"Danielle, understand it is never a waste of time to find out the story of someone's life," replied Ms. Carine. "Every life matters and there is a story to every life." With that, she stood up in an agitated state and said, "You and I will continue our visit next week."

I gathered up my coat and keys to leave. It was already dark when I walked out of her house. Time surely flew by when I was here. I started looking around for the little girl but didn't see her, so I got in my car and drove away. As I was leaving her driveway to get back on the road, I looked in my rearview mirror and there she was. She was standing in the middle of the driveway with the moonlight shining on her. She held up a hand and waved to me.

I slammed the car into park and jumped out of it to talk to her, but the girl was already gone. I'm ashamed to admit that I was too afraid to go running into the woods after her. I jumped back into my car and headed home.

I had a difficult time getting to sleep that night with all of these stories running through my mind. Ms. Carine's life was so interesting and at the same time, so sad. I wondered how long Rosa had worked for her. I didn't like Rosa for the simple reason that she didn't like me. But I hated to think about Ms. Carine not having her help. She was much too old to live by herself. Most people her age were already in a nursing home. When I first met her, she told me she was all alone. I didn't know if she ever had children. I guessed I would find that out when she was ready to share it with me.

I was really grouchy when I got to work that Monday. I hadn't been sleeping well lately, having lots of bad dreams which were forgotten the minute I woke up. Justine had lots of questions, as usual. I told her I asked Ms. Carine about the little girl and that I still didn't have any answers. By this time, my co-worker was as thoroughly engrossed in Ms. Carine's story as I was. We spent our breaks the rest of the week discussing the story of Ms. Carine's life.

The weather Saturday was beautiful and sunny but so cold. I packed up a bowl of chicken and sausage gumbo I had cooked the night before. I didn't want to take advantage of her hospitality, so I felt better bringing a meal or snack every other visit. I had started coming to her house in the mornings because it got dark so early and because I truly wanted to be out of there before the sun went down. That long winding driveway through the woods gave me the creeps at night.

Ms. Carine had a little cough going on this morning and was feeling bad. I told her that if she wasn't well, we could pick up our visits next week.

She said, "Oh no, darling. At my age, I can't afford to waste any time. I never know if I'll still be here." She laughed. "Now, where did I leave off last week?"

"You and Joshua were getting close to his home, and he had just informed you that his family knew nothing about his new wife."

"That's right," Ms. Carine said. "Joshua had just turned my world upside down. I believed that I was coming into a celebration of our marriage, and now I had to face the fact that his family knew nothing about me or our marriage.

"When we rode up the driveway, I could see people working in the fields and in the stables tending to the horses. A young boy spotted us driving up and ran into the house, screaming, "Mr. Joshua is home!" An older woman ran out of the house with a smile on her face. That is, until she saw me. Her smile turned to confusion, and my heart dropped.

"Joshua jumped out of the carriage to embrace her. He turned back to me and helped me out of the carriage. By this time, there was a younger man standing on the porch and an older gentleman walking around the side of the house. He shook the older man's hand and gave the younger man a big hug. Then everyone turned around and looked at me.

"Joshua said, 'This is my wife, Carine. We were married a week ago. She is the reason I extended my trip in Boston. I expect all of you to accept her into our family and give her the respect she is due as my wife.'

"His mother looked at me in shock and horror. She did an abrupt turn and walked back into the house. His father walked up to me and shook my hand. He smiled and said, "Welcome to our family." He called for the maid and gave her instructions to take my luggage and prepare our room, and then he walked away.

"*Well, so much for first impressions,* I thought. *What have I gotten myself into now?*

"Joshua looked at me and said, 'They'll come around. Give them time.'

"He walked me upstairs to our bedroom for me to settle in. All of a sudden, I heard someone running up the stairs, screaming, 'Josh,

Josh, where are you?' The door flew open and a beautiful young woman came flying in. When she saw me, her mouth fell open with surprise and she said, 'Who are you and what are you doing in my brother's bedroom?'

"Joshua said, 'This is my sister, Stella, and this is my wife, Carine, your new sister-in-law.'

"She looked at him then back at me and said, 'Is this a joke? You went away for business and came back with a wife? And, a Yankee at that. What were you thinking? Are you trying to give our mother a heart attack?'"

"And with that statement, she fell onto the bed, overcome with laughter.

"At this point, I was so confused. I really didn't have a clue as to what was going on in this family or what I had gotten myself into. All I remember is Joshua walking Stella out of the room and telling me I was to go and bathe and get myself to bed.

"I know it's silly, but I was afraid of the mermaid on the staircase. I was scared to go downstairs, but that was the only bathroom in the house. So I hurried and cleaned up and went straight to bed and cried myself to sleep. Joshua didn't come to bed that night. I was on my own."

At this point in the story, we took a break to eat the gumbo I had brought. As we sat at the breakfast nook, I told Ms. Carine how tired I was of the dark, dreary weather and how I longed for spring.

She looked at me and remarked, "You should never try to hurry time. It's the one thing we never have enough of. Be grateful for the dark and dreary days, my dear, for without them, you could never fully appreciate the bright, sunny days."

I looked at her and nodded to let her know that I agreed.

I told Ms. Carine that I had seen the little girl again the last time I was here and that it was dark when I saw her, and very cold.

She looked at me in a very thoughtful manner and said, "I will have Rosa go today to our nearest neighbor to try and find out to whom this child belongs."

Rosa looked at me with displeasure. I was causing trouble for her, and she was not happy with me. I told Ms. Carine that there was no need for Rosa to hurry, I just wanted to make sure that she knew I had seen the child again. After lunch, we went into the library and sat before the fire.

Ms. Carine started up where she left off.

"I awoke to someone knocking on my bedroom door. 'Who is it?' I asked.

"'It's Lydia, the upstairs maid,' she replied. 'I've come to tell you that breakfast will be served in the dining room.'

"I said to her, 'I'm not hungry, and I'm not coming down.'

"There was silence for a minute, then I heard Lydia say very quietly, 'Please, Ms. Carine, come down to eat. While you're eating, I'll need to clean your bedroom. The family is waiting for you to begin their breakfast.'

"'Is Joshua sitting at the breakfast table?' I asked her.

"'Yes ma'am, Mr. Joshua is there,' Lydia said.

"'Tell them I am not feeling well and shall stay in my room today.'

"'Do you want me to bring your breakfast up to you,' asked Lydia?

"'No,' I replied. 'I'm not hungry.' *I'll show him*, I thought.

"Joshua didn't come up to check on me until noon. He sat on the end of our bed and placed his chin in his hand and let out a deep sigh.

"'What's the problem, Carine? Do you need me to come and beg you to eat with us? Did I marry a cry baby?'

"I was so confused at this point that I couldn't find the words to express how I felt. The tears kept streaming down my face. Joshua stood up and shook his head in disgust.

"He said, 'You have spent one night in my parent's home and this is how you treat them. You haven't even given them a chance.'

"'What about me?" I said. 'Your mother turned her back on me and didn't say one word. My husband leaves me alone my first night here. By the way, where were you last night?'

"'That's not fair,' he said. 'My mother was in shock finding out that I had married. She will need time to adjust. And for your information, I slept on the sofa so that I wouldn't disturb your rest.'

"'Oh,' I replied, 'I didn't know.'

"'Now you do. Go wash your face and get dressed for lunch. I will wait for you, and we will go downstairs together,' he replied.

"Of course, I did as he asked, and we went and had lunch with his family. I was apprehensive and stressed and wasn't sure how I would be treated by them. His mother nodded at me but didn't open her mouth. His father smiled and said, 'Please come and eat with us.' His brother Robert looked at me with wide eyes and an open mouth. I knew he wasn't mentally stable, but he made me uncomfortable. His sister, Stella, had a small tight smile on her face and looked amused with it all."

Rosa walked in and said, "Ms. Danielle, I have your dishes washed for you to take home."

I looked outside, and it was almost dark. I told Ms. Carine that it was later than I thought and I needed to get home. We made plans to get together next weekend.

When I walked out, it was my favorite time of the day, dusk. The golden hour, as some would call it. The sun was setting quickly, its rays shining on the iron fence. I looked toward the house to see if Rosa was watching me. She wasn't, so I started walking toward the cemetery. I had a morbid desire to see who was buried there.

I kept walking toward the backyard and in the distance I could see the child crouched down in the grass. She was pointing at the gate.

I started walking faster and was about twenty feet away from the fence when I heard a sound. I looked down. A rattlesnake was coiled up and staring straight at me from only a few feet away. I backed away slowly and ran for my life. When I got in my car, I put my hands over my mouth and screamed, hoping they wouldn't hear me.

I was shaking so badly, I couldn't start the car. I looked toward the house, and Rosa was looking out the window at me. She had an amused smile on her face. Did she see what happened or did she hear my scream? I was beginning to think she wasn't a good person, that maybe she was evil. It took me a few minutes to stop shaking, calm down, and drive home.

One of my deepest fears is a fear of snakes. I could have stepped on it and been bitten. I still had shivers running through my body. I didn't know if I could go back there. Well, that certainly put a stop to my curiosity about who was buried in that cemetery. I just knew I would have nightmares that night. I needed to stop thinking about that stupid snake and concentrate on the little girl. How could that child be running around in the woods with snakes everywhere? How was it that no one seemed to notice her being gone? She looked to be about five or six years old. Her hair was blonde, dirty, and tangled. The dress she had on was filthy and torn. I hadn't gotten close enough to her to see more than that.

I also needed to try and figure out Rosa. I knew she didn't like me, but I wasn't sure why. Was she jealous of my friendship with Ms. Carine? Or maybe she just didn't like or trust white people. But she cared for Ms. Carine. I could see that. She was very protective of her and her house. I wondered if she lived there, or maybe she went home at night. I hadn't thought of that. Maybe she had a family of her own. I made up my mind that, like it or not, I would ask her some questions next time I went there.

I was exhausted when I got to work Monday. I had tossed and turned all night long. I dreamt about snakes all night, just like I knew I would. I went over everything Ms. Carine said with Justine. Her eyes were huge and she squealed when I got to the part about me almost stepping on the snake. I told her that I thought Rosa had seen what happened and that she looked amused.

Justine said, "She would have to hate you or be plain evil to take delight in that. If that snake would have bitten you, you could have died."

I said, "I guess you're right. She may not like me, but she surely has no reason to hate me. But my gut feeling was that she did, I just couldn't figure out why."

On my way home from work, I was still feeling jumpy and out of sorts. When I got home, I used a flashlight to walk from my car to my door. Now I was seeing and hearing rattling where there was none. My phone rang as soon as I walked through the door.

It was Margaret inviting me to meet her and our friends for food and drinks. I thought, *Why not? Maybe it will relax me.* It would be fun to see everyone and cut up.

I shared a little bit of what I had been doing the last few months and they all looked at me like I was crazy. They thought it was odd that I was so caught up with an old woman and her life story. Margaret lived in that area all of her life and had never heard of her or the old plantation. That was strange in itself because she knew everyone who lived there.

It did make me stop and think because every time I drove up that driveway, I felt like I had been transposed to another time and another dimension.

My own life ceased to exist when I was there with Ms. Carine, and I always seemed to lose track of time. That in itself was so unlike me. I was usually so aware of my precious time and how I used it.

I was up before the sun on that Saturday morning and I got an early start. Ms. Carine told me that she was up at 5:30 every day. I showed up at her house at 7:00 a.m., but she didn't seem surprised. She offered me breakfast, but I had already eaten. I made up my mind that I would not lose track of time today. I wanted to leave while it was still daylight.

We made ourselves comfortable in the library, and Ms. Carine started her story where she had left off.

"My first meal with Joshua's family was awkward. His father was the only person there who was courteous to me. His mother was still not speaking to me. Afterward, I wanted to go back to my room, but Stella took my arm. She said, 'Come with me. I will show you around your new home.'

"She walked me around the grounds. The yard was beautiful with flowers blooming everywhere. It lifted my spirits and gave me hope that I could be happy here. There were small buildings everywhere. I saw a potting shed, a stable for the horses, and a great big barn filled with hay. There was a huge pond in the back of the house. Then there were the cotton fields, as far as your eye could see. On the right side of the house was a muddy, winding bayou, and there were people fishing on both sides of it. I was amazed and delighted by what I saw there. I had never seen anything like it. *I think I can be happy here,* I thought to myself.

"Stella was watching my reactions to everything she was showing me.

"She said, 'Do you ride?'

"I said, 'Horses?'

"She replied, 'No, dummy, pigs!' Then she proceeded to roll her eyes.

"I replied in a sarcastic tone, 'Yes, I ride horses.'

"She said, 'Tomorrow morning, you better be ready. I'll take you on a tour of this godforsaken place.'

"With that statement, we finished the short tour and she returned me to the front of the house. She turned around and started skipping back toward the cotton fields.

"When I got on the porch, I heard a noise behind the bushes, and I turned my head to see who was there. It was Robert, and he had his pants open with his privates exposed. I gasped and ran into the house.

"I ran straight into my mother-in-law who said, 'What's the matter, Yank? You've seen a man's private parts before, haven't ya?' Those were her first words to me.

"I yelled at her, 'Yes, I've seen my husband's, but I don't care to see his brother's.'

"She said, 'Well, you know he's not right in the head and he is a grown man. Sometimes these things happen. Get used to it.'

Ms. Carine drew her chin down and looked at me over her eye glasses.

I said, "How horrible for you. She sounds terrible."

Ms. Carine said, "She was a terrible, selfish woman. I learned to live with her but never learned to like her. She never called me by my name. She just called me Yank. She always resented that her boy married a girl from up north. I wasn't one of them, and I never would be.

"After that, I went up to my room so I could be alone. There weren't any locks on any of the doors, except the one bathroom. I hated that so much. I wasn't comfortable undressing or laying down for fear someone would burst in. I was on high alert after what happened with Robert. I decided to take time to sit and write a letter to my mother and father. I knew if I didn't write, I would never hear from them. I wondered if they missed me at all. I finished my letter and lay down to take a nap.

"When I woke up, I immediately looked out of the window. The sun was going down, and the room was getting dark. I turned myself over to get out of bed and jumped when I saw my mother-in-law, Mrs. Vernice, sitting in a chair watching me.

"'Is that what you city girls do, sleep all day?' she asked.

"'No,' I said, 'I guess I'm still tired from the long trip here.'

"'Beginning tomorrow,' she said, 'I'll start training you in the duties of managing a household.'"

"'All right, but I promised Stella to ride with her in the morning.'"

"She said, 'We mustn't disappoint little Stella, because Stella always gets what she wants. In case no one told you, dinner is served at five o'clock sharp, which is right now.'

"I got up, fixed my hair, and followed her downstairs. Robert was sitting at the table looking at the floor. Joshua and his father came in together and sat down. I hadn't seen him since noon and had no idea what he had been doing. Everyone was seated except for Stella. Her mother went out on the porch and started hollering for her.

"A few minutes later, she sauntered in. Her hair was all messed up and her face reddened. She sat down heavily in her chair and looked at everyone who was sitting at the table.

"She then looked at Robert and started teasing him, 'Why you looking down, Robbie? What did you do today? Were you a bad boy?'

"Robert started fidgeting in his chair and said, 'No, I was good today.'

"He glanced my way then looked down again. I could feel the heat in my face as Joshua looked at me and then at Robert. He got up and grabbed Robert by the collar and dragged him out of the house. His mother started pleading with him and begged Joshua not to hurt her baby. I felt bad for her because Robert was like a small boy in a man's body.

"I ran outside to ask Joshua to please not hurt his brother, but I was too late. Joshua had him on his knees and he was whipping him with his belt.

"Crying I grabbed his arm and screamed, 'Stop, you're hurting him!'

"He threw me to the side and said, 'Go upstairs, immediately.'

"Of course, I did what he said. From what I was seeing, everyone did as Joshua said.

"I woke up alone that next morning and decided to get up and get my bath before anyone else was up. It was my favorite room in the house because it had a lock on it. I dressed and went outside while everyone was still asleep. It was a very foggy morning, and in the distance, I could see someone staggering toward me. I ran and hid behind a tree, I was afraid it was Robert. It was Joshua and from the sounds of it, he was drunk. *This is interesting,* I thought to myself. *Should I make my presence known or just watch?* I decided to watch and learn instead. I wondered what my husband had been up to and where he had been. I decided to give it some time, then one night I would follow him. I wasn't sure if I was ready to know where and with whom he was spending his time.

"I kept on going and walked past the pond to the bayou. To my surprise, there were two men already fishing. They nodded their hellos to me and turned back to their cane poles. I made my way to the stables so I could check out the horses before the ride. Stella was already there, getting her horse ready.

"She said, 'Take your pick. This one here is flighty and might be too much for you.'

"I never owned a horse and didn't have much experience, but I would never admit it to her so I said, 'He'll do fine.'

"Stella was only three years younger than I, but there was a world of difference between us. I was responsible and had worked hard my whole life. I knew what responsibility was since I was a child, and it had matured me. Stella was a spoiled brat and unlike me, had never worked a day in her life. She was beautiful, and she knew it. She used her beauty on any man who was around her, whether it was her daddy, her brother or a field hand.

"She had long, curly, gorgeous red hair that always seemed messy and flying about. She had sky blue eyes and black eyelashes that were so long, they almost touched her eyebrows. Stella had a sprinkling of freckles on her nose which gave her the illusion of being younger than she was. She laughed and played around with everyone, but her eyes gave her away. They were always cold and calculating, devoid of any emotion.

"We rode around the plantation, and she introduced me to everyone. Then she started galloping past the cotton fields. I was struggling to keep up with her. My horse was ready, but I was not.

"She slowed down long enough for me to catch up to her. Ahead of us was the swamp land I had been told about. Ancient cypress trees overflowing with Spanish moss rose up out of the murky water. A snake slithered into the black liquid that made up the swamp and I shivered as an alligator raised his head above it. Stella giggled when she saw how frightened I was.

"She said, 'If you ever want or need to get rid of a body, this is where you come.'

"I said, 'I can't imagine I'll ever need to do that.'

"She said, 'Well, you never know now, do you?'

"Stella told me the stories of the old slave Diedre who practiced voodoo and who lived all the way in the back of the swamp. She told me about Diedre's potions and spells. I could see she believed every word she was telling me. I wasn't sure I believed anything she said.

"When we got back to the house, Joshua's mother was waiting for me. We had a quick lunch, and then the tour began. She had a big set of keys that she always wore around her waist.

I was very curious as to what the keys opened since there were no locks on any of the doors. One of them was for the silverware. Others were for the closets in various rooms, cabinets in the kitchen and dining room. There were keys for jewelry boxes and linen closets, etcetera. On the second floor was a door that led to a closet. That door stayed locked. She said it went up into the attic and was used for storage. Her advice to me was to stay away from that room. She said there was no reason I should ever need to go in there.

"She informed me that the staff was never allowed to open any of these things. We were to open these doors for them. We had to keep track of whatever silverware was taken out and used.

"There were lists everywhere on what had been taken out that day and when it was returned. I thought the whole thing was time-consuming and a ridiculous waste of energy,"

At that point of the story, Rosa walked in and said, "I've prepared rice and eggs for your lunch."

I found it hard to believe that the whole morning was already gone. I excused myself and went to the bathroom. While I was washing my hands in the sink, I looked in the mirror and saw a young woman lying in the bathtub covered in blood. Screaming loudly, I turned towards the tub, but no one was there.

Rosa was knocking on the door, asking, "Ms. Danielle, are you all right?" When I opened the door, she took one look at my face and said, "Why, child, you're white as a sheet."

I said, "I saw something in there."

"What did you see?" asked Rosa, with a questioning look on her face.

"I saw a woman lying in the tub, covered in blood," I replied, my voice quivering in fear.

Rosa pulled me back into the bathroom, put her hands on my shoulders, and turned me toward the tub.

"Is she still there?" asked Rosa.

"No," I said, with my hands still covering my eyes.

She said, "Ms. Danielle, it seems to me you see things no one else does. Have you always been like this?" she asked.

I said, "No, nothing like this has ever happened to me."

She said, "Well, you sure enough saw a little child upstairs first time you ever came here. You've seen her several more times, so you said. It's funny how no one else has seen her. Now, I don't want you to get Ms. Carine all worked up about nothing. You understand me?" said Rosa.

"Yes," I replied, "I understand."

"Well, get yourself composed and come to the table," said Rosa.

"I'm okay," I said, and I hurriedly walked out before her.

There was no way I was staying in that bathroom alone.

We ate lunch then went back and sat in the library. Ms. Carine continued her story where she left off.

"I didn't have to worry about learning the job of being head mistress for long," said Ms. Carine. "I spent almost every day with Stella, riding horses, talking and wasting time. Every week, Stella disappeared for a couple of days and wouldn't tell me what she was doing or who she was with. We had become fast friends, even though we were complete opposites. I was shy and quiet. She was wild and brazen.

"She helped me take my mind off the fact that I only saw my husband at lunch and dinner. I tried asking Stella about her brother Joshua and why he was so distant.

"She stared at me with a look of amazement and said, 'Why, Carine, I took you for a smart girl. Haven't you figured him out yet?'

"I just looked at her and shrugged my shoulders.

"She said, 'Well, you will. In time, you will.'

"Stella seemed to be bored most of the time, and she was always looking for trouble to get into. She hated the plantation, and spent a lot of her time devising plans to get away from it.

"She didn't plan on marrying anyone local. She wanted a man who was wealthy, and he had to live in the city. New Orleans, of course, was her first choice of cities. But anywhere would do, just as long as it wasn't here.

"It made me sad to think of living here without Stella. She was hard to keep up with and I didn't trust her at all, but she was fun to hang around with. I wished she didn't hate it here. She had a need for excitement and there wasn't anything exciting happening at the plantation. I tried to make things fun for her, but I wasn't much good at it.

"The days that Stella was nowhere to be found and I was alone, I found myself walking around the grounds to see what kind of flowers were already planted. I started pruning the roses and cleaning out the flower beds. There was a yard man named Ross, and he didn't seem to mind me working the flower beds. In fact, he did all the digging and heavy work that needed to be done. Gardening had always relaxed me, and I loved to watch things grow.

"After a few months of pruning and planting, everyone started to notice my hard work. Joshua's father was my greatest fan and walked around the grounds every day to see what was blooming.

"Stella thought I was strange for working in the dirt when I didn't have to. My mother-in-law said she was glad to know I was good at something, and Joshua was amused. I really didn't care what they thought. I was in my element, and it made me happy."

Ms. Carine looked at me and smiled.

"Did you ever ask Stella where she went on the days that she wasn't around?" I asked.

"Yes, I tried everything to get her to tell me where she went. She said that it was best for me not to know. She said it was no one's business but her own."

"Did her mother question her at all?" I asked.

"No, she did not," said Ms. Carine, "Apparently Stella had been raised running around the plantation since she was a little girl. I asked several of the servants if they knew where she ran off to on the days she went missing."

"What did the servants say? Surely they would know what she was up to," I said.

"I could tell they knew, because none of them could look me in the eye. But they refused to tell me. That alone told me it was bad, and that they must be protecting someone, and it surely wasn't Stella," said Ms. Carine.

"How did you know they weren't protecting Stella? Most of them had seen her grow up," I said.

"Because she didn't have a relationship with any of the servants," said Ms. Carine. "It's hard to explain, but Stella was selfish and spoiled. As far as she was concerned, the servants were put on earth to serve her, and that was how she treated them. So she wasn't exactly loved by the help," said Ms. Carine.

"Did you get along with the servants?" I asked.

"I actually got along better with them than the family I had married into," said Ms. Carine. "I understood how hard they worked and how it felt to not be appreciated for their hard work. I also understood that they were people and had lives outside of their jobs. They understood that I was an outsider here and was having a hard time fitting in. But mostly, they loved that I got dirty and worked in the yard when I didn't have to, that I didn't see myself as above them."

"When did you meet Rosa?" I asked.

"She was a gift to me on my 30th birthday," said Ms. Carine.

"You mean she was a slave?"

"Well, not exactly. She was a paid servant," said Ms. Carine. "But she really had no choice in the matter. She was only ten years old and her mother was our cook. My husband decided I needed a companion, one who could be trained early as my personal maid. We've been together ever since."

"That's amazing," I said. "I had no idea. Does Rosa live with you, or does she have a family she goes home to?"

"No, she lives with me. She never married, nor did she have any children."

Rosa came in to see if we needed anything. I checked to see what time it was, and it was much later than I thought. So I said my goodbyes and left.

I got home after dark, which was not as I had planned. I know it's silly, but I was scared to go into my bathroom. I was afraid I would see the woman in my tub, bleeding to death.

Who was she, and why did I see her? Why was I seeing that little girl when no one else was? Rosa might be right. Maybe something was wrong with me.

The following Monday was so busy, I hardly had time to breathe. I wanted to tell Justine what I learned this weekend. I really wanted to tell her what happened when I was in the bathroom. We didn't have time to chat so she followed me home after work. We had a little wine and a long conversation.

When I told her about the woman in the tub, Justine jumped up and said, "Oh my God, you saw a ghost! Someone died in that bathroom and you saw her! I would have run out of that house and I'd never go back. I can't believe you stayed after seeing that. Weren't you afraid?"

"It did scare the crap out of me. I screamed, didn't I? But once I was back sitting with Ms. Carine, I forgot all about it. She makes me feel safe and comfortable when I'm with her. It's hard to explain how I feel when I'm there. I want to hear her story. I have to hear it. I need to know how it ends."

"Just ask her. You have her complete attention every weekend," said Justine.

"It's not that easy. I end up captivated by the story itself," I said, "and I never notice the time."

"Okay," said Justine, "But, what about the dead woman in the tub? When are you going to ask her about that? Thinking about it, I'll bet more than one person has died in that house. Why not just ask her if anyone has died in the house? Then at least you'll know why you're seeing people who aren't there."

I thought about that for a minute and said, "Okay, why not? I'll ask her."

The rest of my week was uneventful. The weather had warmed up, and it was actually nice outside. I spent my evenings outside, enjoying a break in the weather. I also spent my nights thinking about everything Ms. Carine told me and everything she left out. Justine was right.

I needed to ask more questions. She would either answer me or she wouldn't. But what would it hurt to ask?

I picked up my notepad and started writing everything Ms. Carine had told me. This could be my story for the book I always wanted to write. But I wasn't going to share this epiphany with her just yet.

I was more than ready to hear what Ms. Carine had to say about Stella and her disappearing act. I was curious to find out more about her beautiful and younger sister-in-law. I got up early that Saturday morning and headed out to the old house. The temperature had dropped, and it was extremely cold. I couldn't remember the last time we had such a bitterly cold winter. I couldn't wait for the leaves to begin growing on the barren trees. Everything was a dreary shade of brown and gray. Even the color of the sky was a pale grayish white.

As I passed over the old bridge, I slowed down and looked in the bayou. The water was calm and muddy. Nothing moved. I tried to picture it a hundred years ago. I bet it hadn't changed much. I got to the house at about 7:30 a.m. and Ms. Carine seemed happy to see me and eager to talk. We got ourselves situated in the library, sitting before the fireplace and drinking our hot Community coffee.

I asked Ms. Carine, "What was going on between you and Joshua? You haven't mentioned him lately."

She said, "He wasn't around a whole lot then. He worked all day with his father and came around at breakfast, lunch, and dinner. We were hardly ever alone. His family was always around."

"What about at night? Wasn't he around then?" I asked.

She looked at me and thought before she answered.

She said, "He usually took a walk by himself at night to have a smoke. Most nights, he didn't come back until dawn. I always went downstairs to look for him. Some nights, he would sleep on the sofa. Some nights, he wasn't there at all.

"By this time, I imagined that he had a lover, another woman he wanted to spend his time with. He surely didn't spend any of it with me. I just couldn't figure out why he hadn't married her instead of me."

She looked so old and sad at that moment, that I changed the subject back to Stella.

"Tell me more about Stella," I begged. "I'm so curious about her and her secret life."

"Well," said Ms. Carine. "It would be several years before I finally knew where she had been hiding and what she had been doing. When I found out, I wished with my whole heart that I'd never known.

"When Stella was seventeen, she started dating a local boy. He was head-over-heels in love with her, and she treated him like dirt. He didn't care. He followed her around like a puppy. His name was Norman, and his father owned the general store in town.

"She made that poor boy spend every penny he earned on her. He had to work overtime just to make her happy. The thing is she didn't even care about Norman. Stella made fun of him every chance she got.

"I felt so sorry for him, but there was nothing I could do. I tried to talk to her, to show her all his good points, but she just laughed at me. You see, Stella used people, and when she didn't need them anymore, she threw them away. Their feelings didn't matter to her because she didn't feel empathy for anyone. She had a cold streak in her heart, and I never understood why.

"She dated Norman for a year until a cuter, richer boy came along. She broke Norman's heart. That poor boy never got over her. This new boy Cliff was trouble, and he was just what she was looking for. She started drinking and running around with Cliff and his friends. The sheriff came around to warn her father that if she stayed with Cliff, she would end up in trouble. He said that some camps had been broken into, and the evidence was pointing to Cliff and his buddies. Sheriff wanted her father to talk to her before things went too far."

"Did her father speak to her and did it help?" I asked.

"Yes, he tried, but she was hard-headed and used to doing as she liked. She kept running with Cliff until one night, things headed in a different direction."

"What do you mean?" I asked.

"Stella had a smart mouth on her and couldn't control her tongue. One night, she smarted off to Cliff, and he didn't like it. From what she told me, she made fun of him in front of his buddies, embarrassed him in front of his friends. He reached out and slapped her face. He slapped her so hard, she fell against one of those camps they had been breaking into and cut her head open. She was bleeding so badly, she needed stitches. Instead of bringing her to the hospital like he should have, he just dropped her off at the house with blood dripping from her head.

"Joshua took her to the hospital to get her head stitched up then brought her back home. He hit the road, so to speak, in search of Cliff."

"I'll bet he was fighting mad with Cliff hurting his little sister like he did," I said.

"Mad wasn't the word. He was blind with rage. I was praying that he wouldn't find him. I feared that if he found Cliff, he would kill him. I guess God heard my prayers because Joshua didn't find him. Cliff realized how much trouble he was in and disappeared for a while. Joshua went to see Cliff's dad to let him know what his son had done. His dad expressed his sympathy and concern for Stella and promised Joshua that his son would be punished for what he had done. Joshua went to the sheriff and pressed charges against Cliff."

"What happened to Cliff?" I asked.

"The sheriff gave him the choice of going to jail or leaving town. He ended up joining the army. It was the best choice for him because he would have ended up in prison, the way he was going."

"How was Stella handling all of this?" I asked.

"After her head healed up, she went right back to being her sassy self. She said it was her fault for embarrassing him in front of the guys. I told her it didn't matter if it was her fault for getting him angry. He still had no right to hurt her that way. I asked her if she loved him.

"Stella looked at me, threw her head back, and laughed. I'll never forget what she said to me."

"What did Stella say?" I asked.

She said, "Of course, I don't love him. I'll never love any man, but they will love me. I'll make sure of that."

"Did she start dating again after that bad experience with Cliff?" I asked.

"No, Stella kept more to herself at that time in her life. She said, 'Life has just taught me a valuable lesson.'

"I asked her what that lesson was, and she said she would gladly die before trusting anyone again. Then she started disappearing once again during the day. She would head off into the fields after lunch and not come back until dusk

CHAPTER THREE

"STELLA"

"I'm not sure what was going on in her head at that time. Of course, no one knew what she was thinking, except maybe Joshua. He kept an extra close eye on her, making sure she was staying close to home. Those two had a special bond between them. As for me, I couldn't figure either of them out.

"Did you and Stella stay close after that happened?" I asked.

"Not as close as we had been," said Ms. Carine. "She had changed. She was quieter and stayed to herself a lot. I asked her again where she went off to everyday by herself. She said, 'Seriously, I would tell you, but then I would have to kill you.' The funny thing is, I believed her."

Rosa poked her head in and said she had prepared a light lunch for us. We ate in silence for the most part, each of us lost in our own thoughts. Rosa looked at both of us with a question in her eyes.

"My, but you two are serious today," said Rosa. "What have y'all been talking about?"

"Stella," said Ms. Carine, "We've been talking about Stella."

"That would account for it," said Rosa. "It's such a tragic story."

"What do you mean by that, Rosa?" I asked.

She took a deep breath, looked at Ms. Carine and said, "I'll let her tell you that story."

Ms. Carine said, "That story will have to keep until next week. Stella is a very sensitive subject for me. She brings up a lot of emotions and memories that I've kept locked away. Besides, I know that you like to leave here while it's still light outside."

"Yes, I do. I'm not a fan of getting home after dark. I'll get going, and I'll see you next Saturday," I said.

When I got to my car, I turned around and looked at the old house. The sun was going down, and the house was aglow from the rays. I grabbed my camera and took a couple of pictures of it. In the far distance, I thought I saw the little girl walking towards the fields. I wasn't sure if it was her, and if it was, she never turned around.

As soon as I got home, I grabbed my notepad and started writing. I wasn't sure what I was doing putting all of this down, but I couldn't worry about that now. I mean, how often does someone share her life story with you? I needed to start an outline so I could remember who all of these people were. So I started it and worked late into the night and all day Sunday.

The work week seemed to fly by, and I spent my evenings writing everything that Ms. Carine had shared with me. In no time at all, I had written several chapters. I was trying to catch up on everything she'd told me so far so I could come back from the next visit and write what she shared that day.

I woke up on Saturday excited and ready to hear what Ms. Carine would reveal to me about her sister-in-law. I got to her house at about 8:00 a.m. with hot biscuits in hand. She and Rosa seemed to be in good spirits today. Maybe it was because the sun was shining, and it promised to be a beautiful, warm day. Rosa was cleaning house and said she would be going to town for a few hours to get groceries. Maybe this was my chance to ask Ms. Carine to see the upstairs floor of the house.

It was still too cold to sit on the porch, so we retreated to our usual spot in the library. Ms. Carine put her head back on the old rocker and closed her eyes.

She said, "You know I was nineteen when I married Joshua and moved here to Louisiana. Stella was just sixteen. It was only natural that she and I would become close friends. We were so very different in the way we had been brought up. But opposites attract, everyone knows that. I thought she was the most gorgeous woman I had ever seen. I knew without a doubt that she was the most independent woman I had ever met. She thought I was beautiful with my pretty green eyes and blonde hair. Stella felt I needed makeup to bring my beauty out. I had never worn makeup and didn't have a clue how to put it on. So it took several more months before I was ready to try.

"I figured out quickly that she and her mother did not have a good relationship. They were not close at all. Her father, Mr. Sterling, was a dear sweet man, but it was her mother Vernice who wore the pants in that family. I found out that Robert, her older brother, had not been born mentally challenged but had contracted a very high fever at five years old and ended up with minor brain damage. Joshua was born four years later and had taken the spot as the eldest child.

"Stella wasn't born until fourteen years after Joshua and was a surprise, to say the least. She was a tomboy and stayed with the field hands at their cabins more than she stayed at home. She was as comfortable riding a horse as she was walking on her own two feet. She loved exploring in the woods and the swamp. As the years rolled by, I realized that her mother loved her dearly but had her hands full keeping her eye on Robert. He had grown up to be a child trapped in a man's body. He had the urges of a man but only the understanding of a child. She had to watch him every second of every day. He had a bad habit of peeking into other people's windows, and every few months, someone came by the plantation to complain.

"Stella grew up making her own rules, which didn't always make much sense. As far as I was concerned, she should have been gloriously happy. She was a beautiful woman. She was raised in a well-to-do family, and she was fabulously independent. She was also miserable. She was one of those people who were never happy with what they had, always looking for greener pastures. Stella could never explain why she acted the way she did, but I couldn't help wondering if it had anything to do with the days she'd disappeared.

"A couple of years after her violent relationship with Cliff, a man from New Orleans showed up at our door. He was on his way to Shreveport to visit his uncle. His mother had suggested he stop here for a few days. His mother and my mother-in-law Vernice were second cousins. His name was Ned Leblanc, and he was twenty-six and single.

"I could see the wheels spinning in Mrs. Vernice's head. As far as she was concerned, it was a match made in heaven. Ned felt the same way. He fell in love with Stella the first time he laid eyes on her. The deciding factor would be how Joshua felt about it. Ned stayed for a week and promised Stella the moon if she would consider marrying him.

"Joshua liked him and since he was tired of watching his sister mope around, he gave him his blessing. Then he convinced Stella this would be the absolute best thing that ever happened to her. So when Ned left for Shreveport, they were already engaged and wedding plans were being made.

"I was happy for her but heartbroken to lose my only friend in this entire world. I cried my heart out and refused to leave my room. Stella understood how I felt because she too was afraid to leave her home. Stella made Joshua promise her that he would take me to New Orleans several times a year to visit.

"I don't think Joshua expected the emotions that were flowing from me or how much I was going to miss Stella's company. He promised he would spend more time with me and get me out of the house. I was so starved for companionship and so lonely that the thought of not having my one friend around was devastating for me. I also learned the hard way that Joshua made promises but didn't necessarily keep them.

"My mother-in-law put the blame on me that she didn't have a grandchild yet, but she knew who was to blame. She knew Joshua spent most of his nights away from home. She heard the arguments between us when I demanded he tell me where he was spending his nights and with whom. She was also aware that he never answered that question. I wanted to follow him at night to see where he ended up, but I never had the courage to actually do it.

"Stella was my sounding board. She listened in sympathy, but she always ended up changing the course of our conversation.

"She told me that she could and would do whatever a man did. Being a woman was not going to stop her ambitions.

"I laughed and said, 'Why, you have never worked a day in your life! Men are strong and work long, hard hours. They are responsible for keeping their families fed and taken care of. This apparently is something you know nothing about.'

"She looked at me and said, 'But, I would not be one of those sort of men. I would be the man who gives the orders and other men would listen to me. I would be the man in charge, the man who made the most money.'

"I smiled at her and said, 'I truly believe you would be that kind of man and would be no less.

"'But let me remind you, you are not a man. You are a woman—an independent woman, but still a woman.'

"Stella said, 'Yes, how very wonderful for me. I am a woman, but I think like a man.

"'You will never see me cry over some silly man or see me cry because his presence doesn't darken my bed at night. I will do to him as he does to me. No, I will do it to him before he has a chance to do it to me.'

"'Stella,' I said, 'Here you are just engaged and already anticipating the worst from your husband. Clearly, he has loved you from first sight. Don't you love him too?'

"'No,' she said. 'I may grow fond of him, but I will never love him nor will I love any man.'

"I asked her, 'What man has hurt you so badly and broken your heart to make it so cold?'

"'None,' she hastily replied. 'There is not a man alive who is worthy of my love.'

"'But you believe that you are worthy of their love?' I asked.

"'No,' she said, 'I am the most unworthy of all, as anyone who knows me soon learns. This man I'm marrying, let's see how long it takes him to figure it out. So, sweet Carine, don't worry. He will soon tire of my mouth, and I will make my way back here.'

"That night, I had trouble getting to sleep," said Ms. Carine. "I couldn't stop thinking of what Stella had told me. In my own time, I was slowly figuring out Joshua and his sister. They were so much alike, never satisfied with what they had and never letting themselves be happy. They kept the people who cared about them at a distance, never allowing themselves to love or trust anyone. They used people until they tired of them, then they moved on. Joshua understood Stella because she was just like him."

Rosa walked in, and Ms. Carine paused.

Damn, I had missed my chance to ask Ms. Carine if I could go and tour the upstairs. I got up from my chair and told her that it was time for me to go. We made plans for next weekend. I took my time walking to my car, hoping Rosa was busy.

I was scouting around, wanting to see the little girl. I walked carefully around the right side of the house where the formal living room was located. I saw something move in the tree line but it wasn't her. It was a deer. I took a picture of it with my camera, but it was too far away to get a clear shot. I walked around to the other side of the house but saw nothing. I was disappointed as I got into my vehicle to leave.

As I turned my car around, I took one last look at the old house. To my surprise there on the second floor stood the little girl. She was leaning into the window with a look of horror on her face.

Without thinking, I backed the car up and ran to the door, knocking rapidly.

Rosa answered the door and said, laughing, "Oh no, who have you seen this time, Ms. Danielle?"

I said, "It's her. It's that little girl and she's in the house, upstairs by the window. We have to go up there now and get her." I tried to push past Rosa, but she wouldn't let me get around her.

She said, "Girl, you pushing the limit with me. If she's in this house, I will find her. You get in your car and go home. I will not allow you to upset Ms. Carine anymore with this nonsense."

She had a look on her face that frightened me and reminded me that she was anything but my friend. I didn't believe for a minute that she would look for the child, but there was nothing I could do.

I was so wired up when I got home, I couldn't relax. I got my notepad out and started scribbling everything Ms. Carine had told me today.

I finished writing at about 10:00 that night, took my bath, and got ready for bed. I picked up my notes and wrote in, Dubois Family Plantation, Whiteville, Louisiana." I planned to stop by the library on Monday and check the archives to see what information I could find.

A t lunchtime, I went to the library. To my amazement, there were copies of our local newspaper on microfilm which went back many years. All kinds of information popped up. There were lots of names I didn't recognize, but I kept on researching. After a few minutes, one name finally stood out, Aosep, the slave who had carved the staircase. My heart started racing when I saw his name. The article written in the Gazette was old, and it described him as a self-taught master wood carver. The words that brought this article up were Dubois Plantation. It was only a few paragraphs, but I was ecstatic with joy. It had one old photograph of the cotton fields in the background with an old black man sitting under a tree, carving a small piece of wood.

It's not that I doubted anything Ms. Carine had told me, but here it was in black and white, the history of the old plantation. I couldn't make out the date on the old newspaper, but I had the library print out the article. I didn't realize at the time that I was doing research on my first novel.

I woke up tired the next day but excited about what I had found. I shared the information I had discovered with Justine and told her about my sighting of the little girl.

Her reply was, "You have to go upstairs and see for yourself. She could be living up there and those two old biddies would never know. They never go up there, and she could easily sneak in and out of there without them knowing."

I said, "I don't know. Rosa is pretty sharp for her age, I don't believe much could pass her by."

Justine said, "You're talking about a woman who is at least seventy-nine or 80 years old. She can't be that aware all the time. She has to rest sometime. Anyway, it seems to me that it's Rosa who doesn't want anyone upstairs, not Ms. Carine."

"Rosa has told me that it's Ms. Carine who set the rule that no one is allowed upstairs," I replied. "I think Rosa's just doing as she's told."

The rest of my week went by quickly. I spent every lunch hour at the library researching the Dubois Plantation. So far, most of the information I found had to do with what was planted which was cotton. Not much was written about the people who lived and worked there.

I was anxious for Saturday to arrive. Rosa never called me to say she found the little girl. I suspected as much. I'm sure she didn't even look for her. Her excuse would be that Ms. Carine would not let her go upstairs. In my mind, I could still see the look of horror on that child's face pressed up against the window pane. She looked so frightened. What if she was locked up there against her will? I wouldn't put anything past Rosa at this point. I laughed at myself. *Girl, you're starting to lose it.*

I, for the most part, trust people and usually try to see the best in them. Rosa had me puzzled. I wasn't sure if she was a good person or a bad person.

But I absolutely knew I'd seen the little girl in the window. Of this I was positive. I had to question both of them about what I saw and to find out what was done about it.

I awoke to a beautiful Saturday morning. *Here's hoping for a warm day. Maybe we could even take a walk outside.* When I drove up to the old house, Ms. Carine and Rosa were sitting on the porch.

The sun was illuminating both of them, and they seemed to disappear before my very eyes. I put my hand over my eyes and looked again and saw Ms. Carine sitting in her rocking chair.

Ever the gracious host, Ms. Carine asked me if I would like a cup of coffee or something to eat. I thanked her for asking but told her that I had already eaten. I suggested that it was such a beautiful day, maybe we could take a walk around the house. She smiled but didn't look at me right away.

Then she said, "The grounds are still wet from all of the rain. Let's see if the sun will dry it up. Are you getting bored with this old lady's rambling?"

"Of course not," I said. "I love this house, but the yard is still a mystery to me. I'd love to see more of it, that's all." I held my breath as I said, "Do you think it would be possible for me to see the upstairs of your home?"

Ms. Carine smiled and said, "Danielle, you are a nosy Rosie, aren't you?"

I wasn't sure at that moment if I had offended her or aggravated her by asking.

She said, "We don't go up there anymore. It's very cold since there's no heat upstairs. Also, it is a very big part of my story. I promise you that once I get past that part of my story, I will bring you up there myself."

"But what about the little girl I saw up there last week?" I asked.

"Danielle, the door to get upstairs is locked. No one can get up there," she said firmly.

"But I saw her," I replied. "How do you explain that?"

"I can't explain anything you have seen," she said. "You are seeing a child no one else has seen. I can't explain it any more than you can, but let me assure you, she isn't there."

So I let it go, even though I strongly disagreed with her.

"What happened with Stella? Did she marry the guy from New Orleans?" I asked.

"Yes," replied Ms. Carine. "She married Ned. She swore she wouldn't love him or any man, but that didn't stop her from planning an elaborate and expensive wedding. The wedding was held at the plantation and was the biggest event ever held there. People talked about it for months afterwards. Joshua was Ned's best man, and I was the matron of honor.

"She had eight bridesmaids who served in her wedding. I teased her about it and asked her where she had found all of them because I had never met any of the girls.

"She shrugged and said, 'Just girls I went to school with, nothing special about any of them.'

"Ned's two brothers, two of his closest friends, three of his nephews, and of course, Joshua served as his groomsmen.

"There was lots of drinking, dancing and celebrating that night. Everyone was looking at me out of the corner of their eyes, wondering why there had not been a celebration held for Joshua and me. I tried not to let it get to me, but it hurt all the same. I was a good person, and I was kind. I couldn't understand why I had received so little love in my life. Was I just unlovable? I had struggled with that question all of my life. My own mother showed me so little love, and I received even less from my father. Then this man asks me to be his wife and then promptly ignores me after I marry him. It was no wonder my self-esteem was so low.

"Stella, marrying and leaving me, broke my heart into a million pieces. I was lonely, depressed, and afraid. I was frightened of being alone again with no one to talk to, no one to confide in. She was the sunshine in my life, and I didn't even realize it until she was gone. I cried and carried on for weeks after she left.

"Did Joshua spend more time with you like he promised he would?" I asked.

"Oh child, I wish I could tell you he did and we lived happily ever after. But that wouldn't be the truth, and it surely wouldn't be the story of my life."

"Listening to you talk about your past makes me realize what a hard and unhappy life you lived. Sitting here with you, what I see is a sweet and gentle lady, but you're still a lady of substance."

"I've lived so long," said Ms. Carine, "and there is so much distance between my life now and my life then that it almost feels like it happened to someone else. Sometimes, when I'm sharing my memories with you, I feel so disconnected. I feel like I'm talking about someone else's life. There is no emotion tied into the memory. Other times, I slip into the past and I'm there, body, heart, and soul. It is so painful, I can hardly get the words out. I guess what I'm trying to make you understand is that looking back into my life is not always an easy thing for me to do."

"I'm so sorry, Ms. Carine, I didn't know it was affecting you so badly. Are you trying to tell me that you want to stop?" I asked.

"No, that's not what I'm implying," said Ms. Carine. "I'm just letting you know that I haven't started to share the hardest parts of my life with you yet. So, at times, I may get emotional. I just wanted to prepare you for it, if that happens."

"You just let me know when it gets too hard to talk about it, and we'll continue your story on another day," I replied.

"Thank you, dear," said Ms. Carine. "I surely will."

"How much time passed before you heard from Stella?" I asked.

"At first, I received a letter from her every week. She shared all the tiniest details of the people she met to the beautiful apartment they lived in.

"I believe, at first, she was lonely and though she would never admit it, even intimidated. But as time went by, I heard less and less from her. She started to make friends and apparently they went out every night drinking and dancing. I knew this would lead to nothing but trouble. Stella had a smart mouth on her, and she was a huge flirt when she drank. Well, sure enough, after being married for one year, she showed up at our door with bruises all over her body and strangulation marks on her neck.

"Joshua was furious and wanted to string Ned up to the highest tree. Stella set him straight right away about what had really happened. She told him that she had started a romantic relationship with Ned's best friend Brad months ago. She got drunk one night and threw caution to the wind. She left the nightclub with an excuse to her husband, claiming a horrible headache. Ned was in a pool tournament so Stella knew he would be occupied for several hours. Brad offered to take her home, with Ned's blessing. That night, Ned came home and found them together in his home and his bed. He wanted to kill her and would have if not for Brad. He threw them both out of his home and his life. Brad foolishly thought that he and Stella would stay together. He found out that night that this would never be.

"Stella tossed him aside and headed back home that very day. Brad was heartbroken. He had fallen in love with her, only to find out that he had been used and discarded. He had made a terrible mistake and had lost his closest friend for a woman who never even loved him.

"Stella had no shame in admitting to her brother what she had done. She said she was done with men, and she was home to stay. Joshua washed his hands of his sister and wouldn't even look at her."

"What about their mother? How did she handle that?" I asked.

"She screamed and hollered at her, and even called her a tramp. They got into a heated argument, with Stella turning around and accusing her mother of having an affair with a neighbor when she was a little girl."

"She said, 'Mother, don't think I don't remember walking in on both of you, and you being such a good Christian woman and all. You're nothing but a hypocrite, and I hate you and everything you stand for.'

"Well, then Mrs. Vernice slapped Stella across the face and to my surprise, Stella slapped her back. Those were dark days indeed.

"I spent most of my days outside, tending to my plants. Stella rode her horse every morning but didn't invite me to ride along. She was back, but things between us were different. She stayed in her room and immersed herself reading books.

"I think she was trying to escape the mess she had made of her life the only way she knew how. We didn't even share meals together anymore. I could hear the maids complaining about all the extra time and work they had to do because everyone was eating at different times.

It was about this time that I demanded Joshua build a bathroom in our bedroom upstairs. The tension in this house was as thick as custard and I just wanted to avoid everyone in it. I was so tired of having to wait to take my nightly bath. I always took my bath last. That way I could take a long and leisurely soak. Stella knew my routine but she deliberately waited every night and would not take hers until I had mine. I didn't know what kind of game she was playing, but I was infuriated with her.

"I cornered Joshua one evening while he was sneaking off into the dark. I came out of the bushes and confronted him about where he was off to. He wasn't expecting this attack, especially from me. He never answered as to where he was going. Always the manipulator, he turned the conversation back to me.

"'What is wrong with you, and why are you so depressed?' asked Joshua.

"'Let's see,' I said. 'Your sister—my only friend here—has dramatically changed. I don't know her anymore. Your mother is bat-shit crazy, I just try to stay out of her way. Your brother is lurking around every corner doing God knows what.

"'And you, my dear husband, spend every night with another woman. Why did you marry me? What was the purpose? How do I fit into your plans? Please, enlighten me.'

"I thought for a moment that he would confess, but he didn't.

"He took a deep breath and said, 'What do you want from me?'

"I screamed, 'I want you to be a husband to me! I want you to spend your nights in my bed, not hers. I want a normal life. Is that too much to ask? I want a baby. I want a child.'

"He looked away from me and wouldn't meet my eyes.

"He said, 'I cannot tell you where I go, not ever. What else can I do for you?'

"My body had been shaking so badly that my teeth were clacking. Suddenly, I got cold as ice and the shaking stopped. *So this is how it's going to be*, I thought to myself. *Okay, I can play this game too.*

"I said, 'I want you to build a new bathroom in our bedroom, just for me. This bathroom must have a lock on it. While it is being built, I want to go home and see my parents. When the new bathroom is completed, I will return. Do you agree with these terms?'

"He looked at me with a newfound respect and nodded.

"For the first time in years, I felt calm, as if I finally had some control over my life. It felt good. It was a turning point. I would never go back to who I was before. That part of my life as an innocent young girl was finished.

"I finally understood that to survive, I would have to take what I wanted."

CHAPTER FOUR

"CARINE'S TRANSFORMATION"

"The next morning, Joshua sent the carpenters to my room to assess where this new bathroom would be built. I could feel their eyes on me, wondering if I had lost my senses. I could hear Mrs. Vernice screaming at Joshua, insisting that there would not be another bathroom built. In those days, you were taxed on how many bathrooms you had. Therefore, if there was in-door plumbing at all, most houses only had one bathroom.

"I'm not sure what reason he gave her, but the screaming stopped. However, the grumbling did not. Normally, I would have been quivering in my shoes but to my surprise, I was quite calm. An epiphany came to me, whereby I understood that I had quit caring what any of them thought. It was quite a liberating moment for me.

"I started to get my things together for my trip, but I would not leave until the plans were in place for the new bathroom. I had no idea that it would be so complicated. The carpenters went on and on with their concerns about the plumbing. In my most authoritative voice, I demanded that they figure it out so that I could begin my journey back home. I had not spoken to my family since the day I left home, nor had I received any letters."

"But you wrote them letters didn't you," I asked.

"Yes, child," said Ms. Carine. "I wrote them every week and never received a response."

"How sad for you," I replied.

"I never expected them to answer me. In fact, I would have been quite shocked if they had."

"But you kept writing anyway because you were a good daughter," I said.

Ms. Carine smiled and patted my hand and said, "It helped me to write those letters, whether they read them or not. At least I could pretend I had family who loved and missed me. Danielle, I can tell that you had a loving family because you have so much empathy for other people."

"Yes, I had the sweetest and most loving mother God could have given me. We were a very close family with my grandparents, aunts, uncles and lots of cousins living next door to one another. I had a total of eleven cousins living next to me. It was a great way to grow up."

"Why don't you ever talk about your family to me?" asked Ms. Carine.

"You've had such a hard life with your family that I don't feel comfortable talking about how good mine was."

"Please don't feel that way," said Ms. Carine. "I would love hearing about your childhood. Danielle, we don't get to choose our families. We are born into them. What we do after that, when we are grown, is up to us."

I stood up to leave and gave her a big smile and said, "Yes, you are living proof of that."

Ms. Carine smiled at me and said, "If you don't mind, I will have Rosa walk you to the door. I'm suddenly quite worn out."

She called out to Rosa and said, "Come and walk Danielle to the door and make sure you send her home with some homegrown tomatoes."

I told her thank you and followed Rosa to the kitchen.

I said, "Rosa, I had no idea you worked a garden."

She said, "Yes, I have a small garden I tend to. I have done so my entire life. Why? You think I'm too old or something?"

That was Rosa, always spoiling for a fight, especially with me.

"No, of course not," I replied. "I was just surprised."

She handed me the bag of tomatoes, and I left.

When I got home, I sat down for a few hours and wrote everything down. It gave me a chance to go over what Ms. Carine had said. I was intrigued by her life and couldn't wait to hear more. Of course, this would be a one-sided story since everyone she was speaking about was dead. Except for herself and Rosa, that is.

My week was extremely busy, and time flew by. I worked on my notes every night and highlighted topics that I wanted to find out more about. I felt that time was of the utmost importance, and that it was slipping away from me. I was anxious for Saturday and wanted to hear the rest of the story of Stella's life. I wanted to hear about Ms. Carine's trip home and if her parents had missed her at all.

I arrived early Saturday morning and brought boudin and cracklin's as a treat. Another cold front was coming in from the west and with it, rain—lots and lots of rain. Just like always, Rosa had a roaring fire going, but this time it was in the formal living room. I was as excited as a child when I saw where we were going to sit and have our story today. It also gave me a chance to examine the painting of Ms. Carine when she was young.

I said, "This is a surprise. Why did we change rooms?"

"I thought you would enjoy the change in scenery," said Ms. Carine.

I smiled at her and said, "I love your dark and quiet library, and I love this room which is the complete opposite. Natural light fills this room with sunshine, whereas the dark and heavy drapes block all of the light in the library. I admire the light blue velvet drapes and the soft white walls in this room. It gives it a light and airy feeling and a happy vibe."

Ms. Carine smiled and said, "It was a happy room. This is where we entertained. Not that we had much company but when we did, it was in this room. Also, coming in here and confronting that painting is something I needed to do. It will help me to get in touch with that young woman I once was but am no more."

"Do you miss being young, Ms. Carine?" I asked.

"Why, of course I do. I miss the strength of youth. When you're young, you take it all for granted...your energy, your strong arms and shoulders. You think you'll be young forever, but it's a lie. You won't. When you're young, time drags by slowly. You think you'll be a child forever. Then you get to your twenties and you feel like you will always be twenty, but you won't. Watch out for the thirties because time is whispering in your ear. You're not so young anymore. If you haven't started your own family yet, you hear that clock ticking. Before you know it, you're forty! What a hard birthday that is for a woman. Many a woman will deny this birthday and start lying about her age at this time.

"As quick as you blink your eye, fifty is here. You ask yourself, how can I be fifty? How did I get here so fast? You miss the younger version of yourself and find you're stopping before mirrors and examining your reflection more often. It's almost as if you're trying to figure out who that woman in your mirror is. Time was marching on, and you were unaware that your life was passing you by. And then, you turn around for a minute, just a minute, and you're sixty. Something happens at this birthday. There is no denying the decay of aging. No matter how much time you take to apply your makeup or fix your hair, you still end up looking tired. Through all of that, you begin to come to terms with it."

"Come to terms with what?" I asked.

"Coming to terms with the fact that there is a time limit on your life. You come to the realization of how much of your life has been wasted by things that don't matter, that should have never mattered. You are standing face to face with your regrets. You can't go back to right the wrongs, so there is no choice but to move forward. So you do.

"Then you reach seventy and, to your amazement, you're still going strong. You have the inclination that no matter what you decide to do, it can be done, just slower and more carefully.

"How did you feel when you turned eighty?" I asked.

"Eighty was just a number. It didn't mean much to me, just more aches and pains.

"Now, ninety was a conversation opener between the good Lord and me. I just figured that God hadn't made up his mind yet if he was going to let me in those pearly gates or not. Why else was I still here?"

I laughed at that and said, "You remind me of my grandfather. I used to ask him how he was, and he would say, "I'm still here," as if that was an answer."

"It was an answer for him, Danielle. He figured, if he was alive, that's how he was," said Ms. Carine.

I laughed and said, "I guess you're right."

"Let's get back to my story," said Ms. Carine. "I was packed and ready to start the long trip home to see my parents. Joshua swore to me that the new bathroom would be everything I had hoped for. I suspected he was a little concerned I might not come back. He wasn't wrong. The thought had crossed my mind. It all depended on what happened when I got there. I hadn't let them know that I was coming for a visit. I think I was afraid that they would tell me not to come.

"Joshua said, 'That's a long trip you're taking all by yourself.'

"I said, 'I'm not by myself, I have Rosa to keep me company.'

"He said, 'She's just a child. Why don't you take Stella with you?'

"'What are you suggesting?' I asked him.

"He wouldn't look at me but just hung his head down.

"He said, 'The change would do her good and maybe right what's wrong between the two of you.'

"I looked at him and said, 'What do you know, if anything, about me and Stella?'

"He replied, 'I know you two were thick as thieves before she got married and moved away. Now, you never speak to one another other.'

"I said, 'That's not my fault. It's her fault that she keeps to herself.'

"'Maybe she's been too hurt inside to talk to anybody,' said Joshua. 'Perhaps you can help her to heal by taking her on this trip with you.'

"I shook my head and said, 'I wish you would think about me and my feelings sometime. I haven't even let my parents know that I'm coming. So I just show up with someone they've never even met?'

"'Just think about it is all I'm asking,' said Joshua.

I thought about it and came to the conclusion that Joshua was right.

"I figured that more than likely, she would say no, but at least I would have done my duty and asked. To my surprise, she jumped into my arms and hugged me. 'Yes!' she screamed, 'I would love to come.'

"I said, 'I'm leaving in the morning. You need to be packed and ready.' She ran up the stairs, taking two at a time.

"I'll never forget the look on her face when she turned around and gave me a huge smile and said, 'Thank you for allowing me to travel with you, I'll never forget it.'

"I suppose my agreeing to invite Stella made Joshua happy. It had been months since we sat and had dinner together as a family, but that night, we did. For a change, everyone seemed happy and the conversation flowed between us. *Why can't it be like this every day?* I wondered.

"Stella excused herself first from dinner. She still had packing to do. I said my goodnight and started to walk upstairs to my bedroom. To my amazement, Joshua was at my side. He slept with me that night, and our lovemaking was tender and sweet. He held me while my tears flowed. I was confused. Was he here because he was grateful that I was taking Stella with me? Was he here because I was leaving for a long time, maybe not coming back at all? Or was he here because he may actually have feelings for me, his wife, whom he generally stays away from 99% of the time?

"I would have plenty of time to mull this over in my mind. But for this instant, I let myself enjoy the feel of my husband's arms around me.

Stella was up and dressed before me. Her excitement was contagious, and I had to admit I was happy she was coming with me. Rosa was just a child, and it was her first trip away from her mother and her home. She was excited and tearful all at the same time. We traveled by horse and buggy until we got to New Orleans. Then we switched to the train. Stella was uncomfortable being in New Orleans, even for one night. She was afraid to meet up with her ex-husband or someone she knew. We didn't leave our hotel room that night. Instead, we had room service bring us something to eat.

"The trip was long, but we played cards and read books.

"Stella was more like her old self, very talkative and in a constant state of excitement. I tried to explain to her the relationship I had with my parents, but realized that I couldn't explain what I didn't have.

"We got to my parent's home on a Sunday afternoon. My mother was home alone, and my father out, as usual. I was shocked when I saw her. She was so frail. She had grown old, and she was terribly thin. I could tell she was glad to see me, even though she tried to hide it.

"I did something I always wanted to do as a child. I lifted the windows up and drew the curtains open. 'Fresh air is what you need,' I told her, 'and a good hot meal.'

"I instructed Rosa to go and open up the bedroom windows and shake out the linen. I was home, and I wasn't the scared little girl who had left here.

"When my father returned later that evening, he was shocked to find a house full of women, some he had never met. I introduced him to Stella and Rosa then sent them off to bed. My mother was already asleep. She had eaten the stew I cooked like a person starved.

"I handled him like I handled everyone lately, precise and to the point. I asked him if my mother still had help, and if so, who was she and how often did she come in? He was insulted by my questions and informed me that it was none of my business. This was his house, and he did not have to answer to me. That is, until I reminded him that it was my husband who sent him money every month. Apparently, that had slipped his mind.

"The next day, we were up early, so we prepared breakfast for my mother and ourselves. My father had left for work before we had gotten up. Rosa started cleaning the house while Stella kept my mother company. I prepared myself for my mother's maid to arrive. She didn't show up until ten o'clock that morning, and I was waiting for her. I introduced myself and told her to sit down. She was very uncomfortable in this situation and said she needed to get started with her work. I informed her that her work should have been started hours ago. She had been employed here for the last two years. Her mother had fallen ill and she had taken her place. Her name was Nancy, and said that she prepared my mother's breakfast and lunch. She cleaned and washed the clothes, and also did the grocery shopping once a week. I told her that showing up at ten o'clock was unacceptable, and that breakfast was hours ago. The house was filthy with a layer of dust inches thick. I informed her that she was now relieved of her duties. I would advertise for a new maid immediately.

"My mother watched all of this in silence.

"Stella said, 'What are your plans on replacing her?'

"I smiled and said, 'I'll figure it out. In the meantime, we'll get the house back into shape.'

"We spent our first week in Boston doing spring cleaning. The next week, Stella and I went and called on Ms. Nadine. She greeted me warmly and invited us into her home.

"I shared with her news of my family in Louisiana. When I felt that we had established a bond between us, I informed her of the situation with my mother and asked for her help in finding someone trustworthy to hire as her new maid.

"She asked that I give her a little time. She felt sure she could find the right woman for the job. In the meantime, she wanted to throw together a dinner party and introduce Stella to all the eligible bachelors in town. We agreed it could be fun and left to check on Rosa and my mother."

"Did you believe your mother was happy to see you?" I asked.

"I think she was, Danielle, although she would never admit it. Her little girl had become a woman, and it had happened without any of her help. My mother viewed life from her perspective only. Her feelings and thoughts were always placed first. She was a selfish woman. Everything revolved around her.

"She could only base her family's needs as they related to hers. It took me years to figure out that she was a narcissist, the worst kind of mother any girl could have.

"Now, I was taking care of her, not because I had to but because I wanted to. I was nothing like her, and for that reason I was glad. I felt it my duty to see about her, and I was hoping by being here I could finally figure out what made her tick. I was happy that Joshua had talked me into taking Stella along. I didn't feel so alone with her at my side. We took daily walks around town and picked up fresh vegetables at the town market. It worked out well, having Rosa here with me. She kept my mother company and kept the house clean."

"So, did Stella like Boston?" I asked.

"Yes, she loved it, and she loved all the attention she was getting from every man in town. Her spirits were up and for that reason, I was glad, but I was also worried."

"What were you worried about?" I asked.

"I was worried about her drinking and going wild with these young men who adored her. She had a tendency to cause trouble between men, and the last two relationships had not ended well. I felt responsible for her, and I wasn't taking that job lightly."

"By the end of the second week in Boston, Ms. Nadine, true to her word, sent three women to me to interview for the position. I ended up hiring the third one. She was a no-nonsense kind of woman, but she had kind eyes.

"You know, Danielle, eyes are the window to the soul. Life has taught me that you can learn a lot about someone by looking into their eyes. Anyway, this lady's name was Bertha, and she started work immediately. I had a feeling she'd work out.

"My mother still didn't have much to say but she looked better and was putting on a little weight. I hired a young boy to do the yard work and get the garden ready to plant. That way, once I was back in Louisiana, Bertha would have fresh vegetables on hand for meals.

"There was a knock at the door, and Rosa answered it. It was a hand-delivered invitation to Nadine's dinner party next Saturday night.

"Stella squealed in delight, grabbed me by the arm and said, 'We must go shopping. Please don't say no.'

"Nadine had thought of everything and had included my mother and father on the invitation.

"My father laughed when we told him about the party and said, 'Not in a million years!'

"My mother looked interested, to my surprise. I offered her to come shopping with us for a new dress, but she declined. It was fun shopping with Stella. She handed me dresses to try on that I would never have looked at on my own. In the end, I found a slim, cream colored lace dress with pearl buttons that fit my style.

"Stella found a beautiful indigo blue dress that accented her eyes and shimmered when she walked. With her hair the color of ginger snaps and blue eyes that sparkled, she would capture the heart of any man there. I found a light, moss-green dress, plain but elegant, for my mother, just in case she decided to come to the party.

"When we left the dress shop, we decided to go and have a cup of coffee at the cafe on the corner. There were several young men sitting there reading newspapers and having coffee. By the time we sat and made our selection, we were surrounded by them. I never forgot I was married, but I must confess that I enjoyed all of the attention. They made me feel young and beautiful and wanted. I watched how Stella had them all eating out of her hands. She was such a little flirt and very good at it. I hardly mumbled a word to those boys, but I could tell that several of them were interested in me too.

"This was not the place I remembered as my home. Maybe it was always this way, but I had changed. People were so much friendlier than I remembered. Whatever the case, I enjoyed being back home. I needed this trip, and I was glad I had gone.

"When we returned to the house, we pulled out our new dresses for my mother to see. When I took her dress out, her eyes widened in surprise.

"I said, 'Now you don't have an excuse not to come.'

"She didn't say anything, she just smiled. The next day, I sent Rosa with an invitation to Nadine, inviting her to tea that afternoon. She replied that she would be there. When I told my mother what I had done, I thought she would have a stroke. She was upset to say the least. Her excuses were numerous. 'The house is too old. We don't have nice dishes. Lastly, we don't invite people here!'

"'Well, things have changed, and we do now,' I exclaimed.

"Having company forced my mother to get out of bed and get dressed. Nadine was right on time. I made cookies to eat with our tea, pulled out mother's best tablecloth and set the table with her best china. It was awkward at first, but before long, we were all laughing and talking like old friends. I walked Nadine to the door and thanked her for coming.

"She looked at me, held my hand, and said, 'Thank you for inviting me. It's a good thing you're doing for your mother. She looks so happy right now, and that's because of you.'

"We settled into a routine and the household was running smoothly. Bertha was here early every day and had coffee and breakfast prepared for us. She was an efficient housekeeper, and everything had started to shine.

"The garden was planted, and soon there would be fresh vegetables to eat. I now had the boy planting a flower garden and redoing my old rose bed. There was an old bench in the shed which Rosa and I carried out. We cleaned the bench and repainted it a pretty blue color, then placed it in the shade of the garden. My plan was to draw my mother outside to sit and enjoy her garden and the fresh air she was badly in need of.

"The day of the party, we were all in a state of excitement. Nadine sent word that she was sending a carriage to pick us up that evening. I never asked my mother if she had decided to come to the party. As far as I was concerned, she didn't have a choice in the matter.

"As soon as I dressed and fixed my hair, I pulled Mother's dress out and told her it was her turn to dress and do her hair. The look on her face was that of a frightened child. Her pulse was racing, and her face was flushed. At that moment, I took pity on her and put her hand in mine.

"I said, 'I know you're nervous about this party, but you'll be with me and you'll be fine."

"Just as I finished helping her dress and prepare, the carriage arrived at our door. We helped Mother into the carriage and climbed in after her. I had left instructions with Rosa on what to tell my father, should he get home before we got back.

"We were some of the first guests to arrive. Nadine had planned it that way. She thought it would be easier on my mother. We found a small table placed in a corner against the wall and seated her there.

"There were fresh flowers on every table with beautiful, cream colored, lace tablecloths covering the tables. We sipped champagne while Nadine introduced us to everyone. Because of Stella, our table was the most popular spot that night. Stella's dance card was filled, and I don't believe she sat the whole night long. I refused all dance offers until Nadine came and spoke to me.

"She said, 'Carine, why are you not dancing?'

"I said, 'I'm not sure if it's proper, I am a married woman you know.'

"She laughed and said, 'If Joshua were here, he would dance with every woman at this party. You shall do the same.' And with that, she stopped the nearest fellow and said, 'Carine would love to dance with you.'

"While we were at the dinner party, drinking and dancing, Rosa was home having to deal with my very drunk, very angry father. She slipped away from there and knocked on Nadine's door with an urgent message for me. I spoke to Rosa for a minute then got Nadine's attention.

"Nadine said to me, "Go and deal with your father right away, I'll send you home with my driver. Once you've put out that fire, please return to the party. I'll make an excuse to your mother for you."

"Rosa and I returned to the house by carriage. Rosa was upset and said that my father grabbed her by the hair and threw her out of the house. He said she was not to return without his wife in tow.

"When I walked in, he was sitting by the fire with a bottle of whiskey in his hand.

"He looked at me with disgust and said, 'This is your fault, walking in here after all these years, uninvited and acting like you own the place. You forget your place, girl. This is my house, not yours. You take the trash you brought with you and clear out of here tomorrow. She is my wife, not yours. You are turning my wife into a whore.'

"I said, 'First of all, I'll leave when I'm ready to leave, and it won't be tomorrow. Second thing is she is my mother and buying her a new dress and taking her to a neighbor's dinner party is not turning her into a whore. Let me remind you that you were also invited to this party, and you refused to come. Let me also refresh your memory, I'm your daughter, and I spent all of my youth taking care of your wife, my mother. Where were you when I was cooking and cleaning and tending the garden throughout my childhood? Where was the father I needed then?'

"'Don't look at me,' he said, 'Ask your saintly mother where your father was. That conversation is long overdue.'

"'Finally, it's out in the open,' I said. 'So, as I have always suspected, the stories were true. You're not my father and everything that has been whispered about my mother is correct?'

"I could tell by the look on his face that he realized he had crossed a line. It just sunk in that he had gone too far in his drunken state. He stood there confused, not sure of what he had said to me.

'I demand to know. If you are not my father, tell me who he is. Is it the gypsy man who held the séance for her?'

"He shook his head and said, 'I don't know for sure. I don't know if it's true or not. She never admitted it, if it is. But you look like him, with your blonde hair and green eyes. So you must be his. What else should I think?'

"'I don't know what you should think, Father. Yet you kept me and raised me with your name, but not your love. I paid the price of my mother's sin. I was innocent but branded the day I was born. I suffered all of my life for something I didn't do. Children suffer for the sins of their parents. Go to bed, old man, and don't bother me anymore. As of this moment, you are no longer my father. You are no one to me.

"I walked out of the house, got into the carriage, and returned to the party. The rest of the evening is a blur to me. We had dinner and returned home."

"Ms. Carine, what a terrible way to find out! I'm so sorry he hurt you that way," I said.

"Thank you, Danielle, but he verified what I already knew in my heart. It was freeing, in a way, for it to finally be out in the open between us. Next, I was going to confront my mother and give her the chance to come clean and confess her sins to me."

"We all slept late the next morning, and I awoke with my stomach in knots. The party was a success, and everyone there had a great time. My night was ruined by my encounter with my father. I could tell by my mother's face that he had told her what happened.

"She wouldn't look at me, and her hands were shaking. I sent Rosa and Stella to town to run errands for me. I took my mother's arm and suggested that we go and sit outside in the garden for a little chat. She sighed heavily, knowing she was not going to get out of this.

"We sat in the shade, and I started speaking very quietly to her in a soothing voice.

'I know that your husband revealed to you the conversation that he and I shared last night.'

'Carine, he was drunk. He didn't know what he was saying.'

'Of course he knew what he was saying. It was a conversation long overdue. Mother, didn't you think I would have heard all the whispers about you, about me? Don't you think that, as I grew older, I wondered why I had green eyes and blonde hair when you and Father had brown eyes and hair. I wondered why my father treated me like I was a stranger all of my life. I convinced myself something was wrong with me, that I was unlovable.

"'You need to tell me the truth about my father, my real father. I deserve to know who he is so that I will know who I am.'

"'You know who you are already,' she said. 'You are my daughter, and this is your father.'

"'Mother, I don't have the time or the patience to argue with you,' 'You can't run away from your past or your sins. It's time to face what you did, and you owe it to me to tell the truth for once in your life.'

"'You would never understand,' she said.

"'Try me,' I replied.

'My memory is kind of fuzzy. That was a long time ago,' she muttered under her breath.

"Letting out a deep sigh I looked away.

"When I turned back to her, I said, 'Mother, why don't you begin by telling me about yourself. What are the earliest memories that you can recall?' I asked.

"My mother looked at me then looked down at her hands. She very quietly started speaking.

"'My earliest memory is when I was forced to quit school. I was in the third grade and I loved everything about school. I adored my teacher, and I loved writing on the chalk board. I was the eldest child, and my mother had three babies after me. My father was a fisherman and was away for months at a time.

"'I remember him as a big, jolly, man. When he was home, our house was filled with lots of friends, and laughter and drinking. He was usually home for several months at a time.

"'It seemed that just when we had gotten into a routine with him, he was gone again. Mother was happiest when father was home. He did the chores and helped rock the babies to sleep. When he was away, she took her frustration out on me. It was me who had to get up at the crack of dawn to slop the hogs and pick the eggs. I had to wash the clothes and feed the babies.

"'Then she decided that wasn't enough for her. I needed to quit school and stay home to take care of my three sisters. I was devastated. I begged her to reconsider, but her mind was made up. I could read and write, and she figured that was all I needed, me being a girl and all. My father didn't agree, but he knew better than to try and argue with her. I grew bitter with my life and despised my siblings and my responsibilities to them. I met Charles when he started working with my father. I was only fifteen years old. Before the end of the year, we were married. My only request was that we move far away from my family, a request he never fully understood.

"'We started our life together and for a while, I was happy. I had my own house to keep and time for myself. I grew a garden and had fresh flowers for my table. I let Charles know I didn't want a baby anytime soon. Truth was that I didn't want to have a baby, not ever. But I couldn't tell him that. Not that it mattered how I felt. We were married five months when I got pregnant. I wasn't happy but I accepted the fact that I was going to have a baby. The pregnancy was a smooth one. When I was tired, I took a nap. It wasn't as bad as I thought it would be.

"'When I was seven months pregnant, the baby stopped moving. I knew something was wrong, and when Charles got home, he took me to see the doctor. It was then that we found out that the baby was dead. I had to carry that dead baby around in my belly for another month before I went into labor. My body had become his grave. I just knew it was my fault. By the time I went into labor, I was half crazy with guilt. We gave him a Christian name and buried him in our family plot.

"'I just wanted to forget it and move on with my life. My neighbors came by and offered their condolences. I told them I was fine and they didn't need to worry about me. And I meant it, I was fine. I didn't want children. Children equaled work. Three months later, I found myself pregnant again. I knew it was going to happen. When he was home, he never left me alone. This time, I was sick the whole time. They called it morning sickness, but it lasted all day long.

I started losing weight and couldn't sleep. My eyes had black circles under them, and I had to stay in bed. The baby stopped moving at six months and I went into labor two weeks later. We had another boy and another funeral.

"'The doctor told me I shouldn't get pregnant for at least another year. He said my body needed time to heal. Charles took a job and was gone for six months. While he was gone, I rested and took good care of myself. I began to feel much better.

"'By the time he came home, I was happy to see him. I learned while he was away that too much time alone can lead to extreme loneliness. I also came to the realization that I was ready to start a family. I guess I had grown up, being on my own awhile. Charles wasn't sure what made me change my mind about starting a family. He was just glad that it had changed.

"'This time, we prepared ourselves for a baby. I spent my time crocheting baby booties and blankets. He built a crib. We let everyone know that we were trying to have a baby and asked for their prayers. Months went by and nothing happened. Charles left on another job and was gone for three months.

"'This time his being gone was unbearable to me. I felt sorry for myself and blamed him for it. I stayed after him when he returned to find a different job, one where he was home every night. I knew he loved his job, but I didn't care. I made him quit his job where he was happy and start one where he was miserable. He's never forgiven me for it.

"'A month later, I found out I was pregnant again. This time, I had high hopes that everything would work out. The pregnancy was going well. I wasn't sick, and I looked and felt so pretty. We were excited and anxiously awaited our new baby. I went through nine months with no problems. The baby was kicking the whole time. I went into labor, and Charles was there with me. He was a perfect, beautiful baby boy, but he was born with the umbilical cord wrapped around his neck. At that point, something inside of my mind broke and I lost touch with reality. I fought with the nurses when they tried to pull him out of my arms. He was my perfect baby, and I was taking him home. What happened instead was that they gave me a tranquilizer and put me in a mental institution or "the crazy hospital" as everyone called it.

"'I stayed in the hospital for three months. Your father decided that I was back to normal, and it was time for me to come home. I don't remember much about that time. I think I slept a lot. Your father had lost any patience that he had with me and dragged me out of bed. He told me that he wasn't gonna tolerate this behavior anymore. When he got home, his house had better be clean and his supper cooked. For the next year, my days went by in a blur.

"'Charles stayed out almost every night. I was always alone. I wouldn't let him touch me, and the distance between us widened considerably. One night, he stumbled in drunk and had his way with me, against my will.

"'The next month, I missed my period. I didn't tell him or anyone else that I was pregnant. I hid it as long as I could, I didn't even see a doctor. One morning, he was getting up to go to work and he saw my belly swollen with child.

"'He woke me up and said, 'You're with child, and you've been hiding it. Have you even seen a doctor about it?'

"'I didn't have any answers, I just couldn't deal with it. When my time came, I went into labor. He brought me to the hospital to deliver. It was a hard labor for me, but I delivered a fine, healthy baby boy. We named him Matthew. He was perfect in every way. We loved him at first sight. I never knew I could love anyone like I loved that baby boy.

"'We took him home, and he hardly left my arms. He was a colicky baby, and I walked with him day and night, trying to soothe him. The problem was that when he finally went to sleep, I couldn't close my eyes. I was exhausted from a lack of sleep and my nerves were raw.

"'By the end of the week, I finally gave it up and slept. When I woke up, I jumped out of bed because I knew I had been sleeping too long. Why hadn't his cries woken me? I ran to his crib and he was cold. I lifted him and held his tiny lifeless body to my chest. I knew he was dead, but my heart wouldn't accept it. At that moment, I felt my mind begin to break. When your father got home, he found me sitting and rocking the baby.

"'He didn't notice that anything was wrong, at first. He tried to take him from me to put him in his crib. I started screaming and fighting with him and wouldn't let go of my baby. That's when he realized something was terribly wrong with Matthew. He went to get the doctor who gave me a sedative so they were able to pry Matthew from my arms. We'd lost another baby, and had another funeral. I was never the same after that. My husband put me in a sanitarium for one year. He probably should have left me there, but he was determined to bring me home and start our life again.

"'Before I had you, Carine, I had started dabbling in the zodiac and mysticism. I was sure that I was cursed. It had to be the reason that all my babies had died. So I kept going from one fortune teller to the next. I heard someone say that a group of Gypsies had arrived in town. I searched them out and had my cards read. Everything that old gypsy said to me was true. I took money out of Charles' wallet when he was sleeping, and spent it on that old gypsy woman. They all got to know me at their camp because I couldn't stay away. One day, the gypsy woman told me that her son had joined their camp and that he had a gift of speaking to the dead. She wanted to know if I was interested in doing a séance.

"'The first time I saw the gypsy man, my mouth fell open and my heart was racing so furiously that I forgot to breathe. He was the most handsome man I had ever seen. He had light, silver blond hair that glistened in the sunlight. His hair was just long enough to touch his collar. He wore it pulled back in a ponytail. I had never seen any man wear his hair that way, and I found it very sexy. It was his eyes that drew me in and captivated me. His eyes were a deep emerald green, the kind that would inspire any painter to take out a canvas to capture them.

"'I was infatuated with him, I couldn't think of anything else. He listened to me and I told him about the loss of my four baby boys. He said it wasn't anything to do with me, that it was my husband's seed that was cursed. His name was Saban, and he and his people traveled all over the country. They never settled down in one place. His people were made to roam the earth, he said. Always had, always would.

"'One day, I woke up so sick, I could hardly get out of bed. Saban was worried when I didn't show up, and he came to my house looking for me. Charles was at work, and I knew I shouldn't let him in, but I did.

"'He made me a special tea, saying it would ease my nerves and soothe my soul. It did relax me, so much so, that I found myself in his arms. I knew what we were doing was wrong, but it felt so good, I didn't fight it.

"'So, to answer your question, yes, I did commit adultery with this gypsy man, in the home that I shared with my husband. Everything you heard about me is true. I loved him, and I had packed my bags to run away with him. When I got to the camp, they were gone.

"'The tent and their wagons were gone as if they had never been there. I never saw him again. I was a fool for letting him use me like he used women in every town he visited.

"'The next month, I didn't have my period and I knew I was in trouble. Rumors were flying in town, and Charles got wind of what they were saying about me. I denied it, but he was not satisfied until I put my hand on the bible and swore it was all lies. I figured I was already going to hell for adultery. They could just add this sin to the list of reasons.

"'Charles never trusted me again, and our marriage was never the same. Then you were born with golden blonde hair and blue-green eyes, and my lies were revealed before everyone. They just as soon have branded a giant A on my forehead for Adulterer.

"'Charles never said a word to me, but he punished me in other ways. He never helped me with you. He just acted like you didn't exist. I hated getting out of the house, hated the stares and the whispering behind my back. I don't remember much about your younger years, I was taking a lot of nerve medicine back then.

"She looked at me out of the corner of her eyes, checking to see how I was taking all of this in.

"Truth was, my stomach was in knots, and I felt queasy, but there was no turning the clock back now. The truth always comes out.

"'Finish your story, Mother,' was all I could say to her.

"'As I was saying, the doctor had me on an awful lot of nerve medicine back then, so my memory is a little hazy. People can be cruel to one another, and children are the ones who suffer the sins of their parents. It wasn't right what I did, and it wasn't right for others to make you bear the weight of my mistakes. I just want you to know, Carine that I'm aware of what a terrible mother I was to you, and I'm so sorry. I have borne the weight of this guilt all of my life, and I'm tired now. I just can't carry it any longer.

"'I didn't say anything to her. I just gave her my arm and helped her inside the house," said Ms. Carine. "At that moment, I just wanted to be alone, to absorb the weight of my mother's confession. I instructed Rosa to watch over my mother while I took a long walk along the river.

"It was easier now to imagine my mother as a young woman, alone and confused. Why had she stayed silent all these years, when I needed her most? But after all these years, she had finally acknowledged what a horrible mother she had been to me, and I had received an apology. Better late than never, I suppose. It was more than I expected from her.

When I got back to the house, all was quiet. Mother was sleeping and Rosa was in the garden. Stella was nowhere to be found.

"'Where's Stella?' I asked Rosa.

"'A nice looking young man came to call on her and they left to take a walk,' said Rosa.

"I was too exhausted to worry about Stella and what she was up to. I went to my room to take a nap. I slept a lot longer than I anticipated. When I woke up, it was late afternoon and Stella still wasn't home. I started to worry. By eight that night, she still hadn't shown up, and I had a bad feeling in the pit of my stomach.

"I sent Rosa to Nadine's and asked her for help in locating Stella. I didn't even know which man she had left with. I knew if anyone could help me, it would be Nadine. She sent word back that she had someone going to look for her.

"At midnight, Stella came stumbling home with bruises all over her face and body. She was hysterical and not making any sense. I sent Rosa to fetch the doctor. Nadine showed up and sent her driver to get the police.

"Stella's mouth was bruised and bleeding, and she had marks around her neck and wrists. Her dress was torn, and her hair was tangled. She wouldn't stop crying and then she started throwing up. The doctor gave her a sedative and told us to clean her up. He informed the police chief that he would have to wait until the next day to question her.

"I sat up with her all night long. At first, she moaned and groaned in her sleep. Then she started crying, and that progressed into screams of terror. I held her tightly and tried to comfort her as best I could. Eventually, we both slept, me with my arms wrapped around her, trying my best to comfort.

"When we awoke that morning, the chief was already at our door. Stella could hardly move. As I helped her to dress, I gasped at the black and blue marks all over her thighs. She was hurt very badly. The chief told her to take all the time she needed, he was here to help.

She told him she wasn't sure where to start. In pity, he looked at her and told her to start at the beginning.

"Very quietly, not meeting his eyes, she began her story. She said that a young man she had met at the cafe came by the house yesterday. He asked her to take a walk around the city with him so he could get to know her better. They walked awhile then stopped for a cup of tea at the cafe where they first met. A couple of his friends stopped by and visited with them.

"His friends invited them to come over to their place. They were having a party. She told him she couldn't go because she hadn't told me where she was or who she was with. He understood and said he would walk her back home.

Instead, he took a different path to bring her home.

"Stella looked at me with eyes that were haunted and told me they'd had a plan all along, that she'd been stupid and fell right into it.

"They beat her then took turns raping her, over and over, until she passed out. She woke up on the street, left there like a piece of garbage.

"Exhausted, she laid her head down and began crying. I told the chief that was enough for today. She needed to rest."

Rosa walked in and said, "My, you two have been at it for a while. Miss Danielle, do you realize it's past 7:00 o'clock? It's already dark outside."

I jumped up and said, "I had no idea it was this late. I must be going." I was so caught up in Stella's ordeal that I never realized what time it was.

Ms. Carine smiled and said, "We'll continue next week. Come early, and Rosa will have a hearty breakfast for us to enjoy."

Rosa walked me to the door and said, "You not afraid of the dark, are you?"

I shook my head, but what I wanted to say was, *I'm only afraid of the dark when I'm here.*

As I was driving away, by force of habit, I looked toward the graveyard. I saw the little girl walking past it into the dark. At that moment, she turned around and looked at me. Her eyes and mouth were opened wide and she had a look of death about her. I was startled by her appearance and jumped in my seat. I took off so quickly that my tires threw gravel everywhere.

When I got home, I had the jitters. What if she had followed me home? I locked my door and closed the curtains. I didn't want to look outside. I was afraid she was out there. I went to my desk and started writing down everything Ms. Carine had shared with me.

I spent all day Sunday writing. I wasn't sure how my book would turn out, but for the time being, I had to get it down. Right now, I was learning about Stella's life, but the true mystery for me was the little girl. If Rosa and Ms. Carine were telling the truth and I was the only one seeing her, then her presence on this Earth might be in spirit form only. *Why was I the only one seeing her?*

CHAPTER FIVE

"STELLA'S ORDEAL"

My week flew by quickly. I worked all day and wrote at night. On Friday evening, Margaret came by to visit. I could tell she had something on her mind.

I said, "What is it? I can tell something is troubling you. What is it that you need to say to me?"

She laughed and said, "Okay, your friends are worried about you. We don't see you anymore because you're spending every weekend with this old lady. It's like you're obsessed with her and her life. We don't understand the attraction or what you are getting from this. I've questioned some of my older relatives about Ms. Carine. They remember hearing about this family. They heard about this family when they were children. This means they have been dead for years. No one knows Ms. Carine and cannot locate this old plantation home that you go to every week. Don't you think that's strange?" asked Margaret.

"Yes, it is odd that no one knows her," I replied. "Although, I know that she is reclusive and doesn't get out much. She's old and has outlived all of her family. It's hard to explain how I feel when I'm with her. I have always felt the need to write but never could.

Now I have a story—her story—and I'm writing feverishly every day."

"I'm happy you're finally writing," said Margaret. "Do you have to go every weekend, though?"

"Yes, because time is limited. She's not getting any younger," I replied. "I feel its urgent to write her story down before it's too late."

"Is there anything else you want to tell me?" asked Margaret.

"Okay, have you been talking to Justine?" I asked.

Margaret looked at me and smiled sheepishly.

"Yes, I did talk to her, and she told me about the little girl you keep seeing. She also told me about what happened in the bathroom and about the snake. Why haven't you told us about any of this?"

"I don't know, I guess I'm afraid you guys will think I'm losing it."

Margaret sighed and looked at me.

"Why aren't you worried about what Justine thinks? You don't have a problem sharing all of this with her."

"It's different. I see her every day, and she's interested in what I'm doing. I have to tell someone. I spend eight hours a day with her every day. That's the only reason," I said.

"Okay," said Margaret. "Let's call a truce. From now on, you have to open up to your friends. We're the ones who know you best and love you. Don't keep what's going on only to Justine, keep us in the loop too. Agreed?"

"Yes, I agree. I'll keep in touch and tell you what's going on so you don't worry. But I'm not going to stop until I have the whole story. You have to promise me to stop looking at me that way."

"What are you insinuating?" asked Margaret.

"You look at me like you think I'm losing my mind. Be assured, I haven't. I am aware how strange this situation is."

"Okay, as long as you're aware that this is not a normal situation, I feel better about it," said Margaret.

I walked her to the car and promised to keep in touch. I finished writing what Ms. Carine and I had discussed last week. I was anxious to hear the rest of Stella's story.

When I woke up Saturday morning, the sun was shining, but it was still bitterly cold outside. I bundled up and made my way to the old house. When I got to the bridge, the sun's rays were bouncing off the bayou. This would make a terrific picture, I thought. So I pulled over to the side of the road. Stepping out of the car with my camera, I positioned myself to get a deep view of the bayou. I took the shot and vowed to get the film developed Monday. It seemed to be a perfect shot, and I was extremely happy with it. I couldn't wait to see the print.

I made my way to Ms. Carine's and still managed to arrive early, as she had suggested. Rosa had a huge breakfast waiting for us and a fire going in the formal living room. That we were back in this room surprised me.

Ms. Carine smiled and said, "I want to finish Stella's story in this room."

"Oh, that's just fine with me," I replied. "I love this room."

"So did she," said Ms. Carine.

We made ourselves comfortable, and Ms. Carine began her story.

"The police were looking for this young man who had said his name was Evan. The only problem was that no one knew anyone by that name. They spoke to the person working at the cafe that day. He remembered them being there but was not acquainted with the man who was there with Stella.

"At the same time, Stella wasn't doing well and didn't want to get out of bed. She just lay there, curled up in the fetal position with tears streaming down her face.

"I wrote to Joshua letting him know what had happened to his sister. I needed to get her back home, but she wasn't in any state to travel at the moment. I put Rosa in charge of watching Stella, and I went alone to the cafe hoping to meet up with someone, anyone, who might have been there that day. I didn't have any luck. No one would speak to me.

"When I got home, Rosa was at the front door waiting for me.

She strongly suggested I speak to Stella because she was 'talking crazy talk.' When I pressed for more information, she told me Stella was talking about killing herself.

"I assured Rosa that wasn't going to happen, then went and sat by Stella's bedside. She was so pale and quiet.

She looked at me with tears in her eyes and begged me to take her home.

"I gave her a hug and took her hand in mine. I told her that she was going to be okay, but I didn't know if I believed it. Stella's mouth often gotten her into a lot of trouble, but she didn't deserve this. No one did. I realized at that moment that I loved her like she was my own sister. Since I had never had siblings, it was a new feeling for me. With that feeling came a loyalty to her, a sense of protection toward her. We were only three years apart, but I felt eons older.

"The chief came by one day and said that they had been questioning all of the regulars at the cafe. Not one person knew anything about this group of men. He stressed the fact that he wasn't giving up and that she shouldn't either.

"I received a letter from Joshua later that week. He informed me the new bathroom was finished. He demanded that I bring Stella home immediately. He reminded me of our agreement. What he didn't know was that I had missed two periods since I was here. I didn't think anything of it because my periods were always irregular, and this wasn't the first time it had happened. But in the last few days, I was nauseated in the morning and my breasts were tender. I was having trouble acknowledging that I might be pregnant. A part of me was ecstatic, but another part of me was cautious. Praying for a normal relationship for all these years and not having one, why now?

"So plans were underway to return to Louisiana. I had mixed feelings about leaving Boston. On one hand, it had been a hard trip coming back here. Finding out the truth about who my real father was had boggled my mind. Knowing I was a bastard child of a traveling gypsy wasn't helping my self-esteem. On the other hand, finally feeling like my mother and I were at last communicating was a gift I would always treasure. I dreaded leaving her, not sure that I would ever see her again."

CHAPTER SIX

"RETURNING TO LOUISIANA"

"Both Stella and Rosa were anxious to leave Boston and return home to Louisiana. They had enough of the north and were ready to head south. Our bags were packed, and we were ready to go. I took my mother's arm and led her outside to the little bench in the garden. We sat awhile in silence, each lost in our own thoughts.

I offered her to come and live with me in Louisiana. I knew that the Dubois's would welcome her and so would Joshua.

She looked at me in surprise and shook her head.

She said that her place was with her husband, just as mine was. He had stayed by her side and she owed him.

I told her that she didn't owe him a thing. He was never there for her. It was me who took care of her all of these years. If she owed anyone, she owed me.

She told me I didn't understand, and that I never would. She said that there were bonds between a husband and wife and they should never be broken.

I told my Mother that I didn't understand and that I knew nothing about bonds between a husband and wife, not in my marriage anyway. I said if I was ever lucky enough to be a mother, my bond would be with my child.

I thought about sharing my news with her about my suspected pregnancy. Then I decided against it. It wouldn't change her mind about coming with me. I gave her my arm and walked her back into the house.

I thanked her for having us in her home. I let her know that the invitation I had extended still stood. I told her to take care of herself and that I would have Nadine keep an eye on how she was doing. I assured her that if she needed me, all she had to do was contact Nadine.

I hugged her, but she didn't hug me back. I would never understand this woman, this mother of mine. I swore to myself if I was lucky enough to have a baby, I would hug and kiss that child every day. I would not let a day go by without showing her how much I loved her.

Rosa and I got Stella into the carriage and loaded up our bags. Stella was frail, a shadow of her former self. I was worried about her making this long trip back home. But she was adamant about leaving this place now, not later. She had nightmares every night. She was afraid of this group of men, scared that they would come back to finish her off. They knew that she would recognize them and turn them in to the authorities if she crossed paths with them again. It was then that I decided to purchase a gun to carry with us. I needed to be prepared if anything should happen on the way back home.

Stella held on to me for dear life until we were far enough for her to feel safe. I wasn't looking forward to this trip back south and I prayed for our safety. The heaviness of the gun in my purse reminded me of the constant danger we were in and what I may have to do to protect my sister-in-law.

The beginning of the train ride was uneventful, and Stella slept through most of it. One evening, as I was sitting alone in the dining car, a woman about my age approached me and asked if she could sit with me. She had huge, dark brown eyes and a head full of black shiny curls piled high and secured in a bun. She was a bundle of energy, and every time she spoke, she shook her head and a few curls came loose causing her to have a disheveled but nevertheless cute appearance.

Her name was Bunetta and she was from Natchez, Mississippi. She was married to Dr. Henry Butler, and he was at home anxiously awaiting her return. She had been to visit her old aunt for a few weeks in Tennessee and had left their three young sons in her husband's care. She hooked her arm into mine and pulled me close to her and whispered in my ear.

In her cute southern accent she said the only reason she was able to get away all by her lonesome was because the good Dr. Butler was betting on the fact that she would inherit all of her aunt's money. He believed her going to take care of her aunt while she was lying on her death bed would somehow guarantee Bunetta first place in her aunt's will.

I gasped and told her, that of course that's not why she went to see her dear aunt. She went because she loved her and it was the right thing to do.

Bunetta lowered her eyes and giggled a little and told me that of course that was exactly why she rushed to her side. She confided that poor old woman had no one to count on except her hired help. She had never married and was dying a spinster. Her Aunt Dean was three years older than Bunetta's mother whose name was Charlotte. Charlotte had always warned her older sister about the disadvantages of not getting married and not having children, thereby not having anyone to care for her in her old age. She told me that her Mother would tell her Aunt Dean that just because she was younger than her, she would not be the one to take care of her when she got old. Charlotte constantly reminded Dean that she was the one who made the decision not to get married and have children. Bunetta said her mother was always right, and so even though she was younger by three years she still managed to die before her little sister, thus making her prediction come true. Her little sister Dean would die a spinster and childless, with no one to care for her.

"I didn't know what to think about Bunetta. She was personable and friendly, and I knew we would become fast friends. She had a high pitched, giggly laugh that made me want to giggle too. By the end of our first meal together, we felt like we had always been friends. Before our first meal was consumed, we were already making plans to take turns visiting one another.

"The next morning, Stella still didn't feel well enough to get dressed and eat breakfast in the dining cab. So I ordered breakfast for her and Rosa to eat in. I, myself, went to the cab to eat, and Bunetta was there waiting for me. Her eyes were sparkling with mischief, and I wondered what she was up to.

She told me that we would take our time and try everything on the menu. She asked me what I thought of her proposal.

I told her that it was ridiculous, I couldn't eat that much and it would also be very expensive meal!"

Bunetta laughed and asked me if I always did what was reasonable? I took a deep breath and said that I tried to.

I remember Bunetta's eyebrows arching up and her saying it was fate that we had met. She said she never did what was reasonable, and that was the reason she had always been considered a handful! Besides that, she said her life was never boring and promised me that when I spent time with her my life would be anything but boring. Her husband was rich so she could pay for everything. I had nothing to worry about. I figured my husband was worth a pretty penny too, running that big old cotton plantation, but if he was rich I would be the last to know.

So we tried everything on that menu and ate until we couldn't anymore. We laughed the entire time, and I'm sure the people on that train thought us quite mad. All of a sudden, I felt ill and ran to the restroom to vomit. She followed me to make sure I was okay.

She asked me how far along I was.

I looked at her perplexed and asked, How did you know? I haven't told anyone yet.

She told me that she had three children under the age of six. How could she not know?

She wet a washcloth with cold water and laid it across my

forehead. She looked at me and started giggling, and said it was no wonder I was so hungry. I was now eating for two!

As soon as I felt better, we went to Bunetta's room and played rummy. It was a game we were both familiar with. We started talking, and I told her about Stella and everything that had happened to her. She was intrigued by my story and wanted to meet her. I hadn't said anything to Stella about my new friend. I had held that information back, and I wasn't quite sure why. I made an excuse for tonight and promised Bunetta that I would set something up for tomorrow."

At that moment, Rosa knocked on the door and said, "I've prepared soup and sandwiches for you and Ms. Danielle to eat. It's time for you two to take a break."

We got up, stretched, and went into the kitchen to eat what Rosa had prepared. I excused myself and went to the bathroom even though I was afraid of that room. I reassured myself that everything would be okay. There was no one in that bathroom but myself but I still kept my eyes closed while sitting on the toilet and was too afraid to open them. Scolding myself for being ridiculous, I opened my eyes and exhaled deeply. To my relief, no one was there. I walked over to the sink and turned the faucet on to wash my hands.

Unexpectedly, I felt a deep chill run through my body. I slowly looked up into the mirror and there, in the corner of the room, stood a woman. She was dripping wet and covered in blood.

Her body was slumped over, with her head hanging down and her hair wet and stringy was covering her face. Water and blood were dripping from her long, wet curls. She started to lift her head up to look at me.

I held onto the sink because my heart was racing so fast, I thought I would pass out. I turned around quickly to face her, but she was gone. As I rushed out of the bathroom I ran right into Rosa.

"Oh no, Ms. Danielle, what has happened now?" asked Rosa.

I put my hand over my heart and tried to catch my breath.

I said, "In the bathroom, there was a lady standing in the corner.

She was dripping wet and covered in blood. I know you don't believe me, but it's true!"

Rosa asked, "Is she still there?"

I sighed deeply and said, "No, I saw her in the mirror. When I turned around, she was gone."

Rosa said, "Come now, Ms. Danielle. I'll go with you into the bathroom. If this woman was there, then the floor should be wet and covered in blood. Do you agree?"

I nodded and followed her into the bathroom. The floor was dry and there was no sign of blood.

Rosa said, "I don't understand what's going on in your head or why you're seeing these things, Ms. Danielle. But I will reiterate with you the necessity of not upsetting Ms. Carine with this nonsense. She is an old woman, and her heart is weak. It is my responsibility to take care of her, and you had better understand. I will not let you upset her again."

"I understand that you want me to lie and hide what is happening here from Ms. Carine," I answered.

"Little girl, you are pushing my buttons and believe me, you don't want to do that," said Rosa.

With that statement, she turned and walked away. Well, I thought. That was a threat, and I will take it as one.

Ms. Carine walked into the room and headed back into the formal living room. I followed her.

"Ms. Carine, do you have a portrait of Stella?"

Ms. Carine said, "Yes, I do. I have several pictures of Stella. They've all been put away. I'll see if Rosa can locate them for you."

"Are you ready to get back to the story? said Ms. Carine.

I nodded and sat down. Ms. Carine began her story where she had left off.

"Stella wanted to know where I had been and what I had been doing. I told her about my new friend Bunetta. I was surprised and a little disappointed when Stella showed little to no interest in meeting her. She wasn't ready to have company and preferred that I go and meet my new friend in her cab. I knew that Bunetta would be disappointed and maybe even insulted. There was nothing I could do or say to change Stella's mind. I ordered food for Stella and Rosa and went to Bunetta's room to visit.

"When I got to Bunetta's room, I could hear voices and giggling. I knocked on her door, and everything got quiet. The door opened up and I saw a man sitting on the edge of her bed.

I gasped and said, "I'm sorry," and I turned to leave.

Bunetta laughed and said for me not to be silly. This was Jim, an old friend of hers and that he had just stopped by for a visit.

This man called Jim smiled and said how very nice it was to see her again and that it was a pleasure meeting me.

After he left, I looked at Bunetta and asked, "Doesn't your husband mind you having men in your bedroom?"

She smiled and said that what he didn't know didn't hurt him. She told me to lighten up that I was much too young to act so old.

"I knew her behavior was wrong, but somehow she made being bad seem like fun. I really liked her, so I pushed away any negative thoughts about her out of my mind. We were inseparable on that train, and I couldn't remember ever having so much fun. I did feel bad about ignoring Stella and Rosa the entire trip back home. I just pushed that guilty feeling aside.

"When we reached New Orleans, Bunetta and I hugged each other tightly and exchanged addresses. We had already started making plans to visit each other in the near future. Stella and Rosa were angry with me for ignoring them, and both were sulking. We stayed one night in the city and left the next morning for home. It was a very quiet trip with everyone wrapped up in their own thoughts.

"By the time we got home, my nerves were frazzled from all of the tension between us girls. The fact of the matter was that I was throwing up every morning and had actually lost a few pounds. Joshua and Mrs. Vernice were sitting on the porch when we got there. Stella was the first one out of the carriage, and she passed by both of them without a word. They both looked at me with a question in their eyes. Of course, this would be my fault. I had forgotten that everything that went wrong was blamed on me. I was too tired to worry about them. They already knew how hard-headed Stella was. If they couldn't handle her, they shouldn't expect that I could.

I explained to Joshua that we were exhausted and needed rest.

CHAPTER SEVEN

"EXPECTING"

"I went straight up to my room and inspected my new bathroom. It was wonderful. Everything I had hoped for. When I turned around, Joshua was standing there staring at me.

He asked if I approved of my new bathroom. He was quite pleased with himself, so much so, you would have thought he built it himself.

"I told him it was lovely and I thanked him for his gift.

He told me that I looked different and noticed that I had lost a few pounds.

I figured I might as well tell him now.

I told him he was quite observant and I was pregnant with his child.

He looked at me with surprise and said after all these years we're going to have a baby. He thought it was incredible news and he looked happy.

Part of me wanted to share his happiness. The other part that had been hurt and ignored by him for so long wanted to show him how that felt.

He noticed my look of anger and asked me why I was staring at him.

"I told him that if we had a normal marriage, where my husband spent his nights with me instead of God knows where or with whom, we may have three or four kids by now. I said my friend Bunetta had three little boys and hadn't been married as long as we had.

He asked me who Bunetta was and where did I meet her?

I told him not to change the subject but I shared with him how we met. I told him that she was a wonderful person and lived in Natchez, Mississippi with her three sons and her husband Henry.

I informed him that her husband was a doctor and had a practice in their home and she had invited us to come and visit them after the baby was born.

I had his attention all right and he wanted to know how my new friend knew about the baby before he did.

"I told him that she saw me throwing up one day, and she knew right away, because women know these things.

He looked at me and smiled.

He told me that things would be different now. He said for me to enjoy my bath and that he would see me in a little while.

"I started my bath and added the scented bath salts to my water. I wondered who had placed these in here. I knew it wasn't his mother, and I couldn't see Joshua buying these.

"This was heaven, my own private bathroom. I took a luxuriously long bath and climbed into bed for a much needed rest.

"I fell asleep as soon as my head touched my pillow. Through my deep sleep, I could hear Stella sobbing in the night. I knew I should go to her, but I was so tired. I fell back asleep. At some point in the night, I felt Joshua slip into bed and run his hand over my belly. I fell back into a deep sleep.

"I awoke to the smell of bacon frying and biscuits in the oven. I was so hungry that I felt weak. I once again admired my bathroom before I hurried to breakfast. I was the last one to the table, but there was plenty of food left. Everyone laughed at how hungry both Stella and I were. I could tell that Joshua had already shared the news of my pregnancy with his mother. You would have thought that that she was the one expecting. Her face was positively aglow.

She looked around the table and said that it was just like she always thought, that northern cooking couldn't hold a candle to the food down south. She asked if we girls ate anything at all while we were gone.

"I could tell she was just picking at me. I was going to have her first grandchild. All was good between us for now. Besides biscuits, eggs, and bacon, there was boudin and cracklings. It was a feast and all of us enjoyed it.

Joshua surprised me by taking my hand and telling his family that he and I would like to share our happy news with all of them. He then told them that we were expecting our first child.

"I could see first the amazement on my father-in-law's face and then the realization of his first grandchild. He and Mrs.Vernice came and hugged both Joshua and me. It was my first hug from either of them and very awkward. But it was also a nice feeling, a feeling of finally belonging here after all these years.

"Stella was the only one who wasn't smiling or offering any congratulations to us. She excused herself and went up to her room.

"As we left the breakfast table, I quietly told Joshua that he and I needed to talk privately about what had happened in Boston.

He told me we would not discuss it today. He said that today was a day of happiness for us to share with our family and friends. We would talk about this tomorrow. He said that his mother had invited some of his cousins over for cake and coffee. She wanted to share our good news with some of his family.

I told him if he had been a husband to me all of these years, this would have happened a long time ago.

Joshua asked me if it was my intent to ruin the day by arguing about the past. I told him not at all and that I would keep my mouth shut about the past and try to imagine our future instead. I told him that today was a new beginning for us. He looked at me and smiled and nodded yes.

Being overly nice he told me if I wanted to go upstairs and rest, his cousins would be here about ten o'clock.

"I said yes, I believe I will go and lay down for a little while. Instead, I went upstairs and knocked on Stella's door.

I heard her mumble, and ask who is this and what do you want?

"I whispered to her, it's me, and I said please let me in.

She said for me to tell her what was on my mind.

"Are you okay?" I asked.

Stella looked at me and shrugged her shoulders.

She asked me what was the matter, was I missing my good friend Bunetta? Did I not have anyone to whisper and share my silly stories with? I had proved to her that I was not her friend by abandoning her on the trip back home. I of all people knew what she had been through, and yet I left her alone to cope with it. She would not forget nor forgive me, so I shouldn't bother asking.

I took a deep breath and told her that I had not come here to ask for her forgiveness. I was sorry if I hurt her feelings on the trip back, but I was not sorry that I made a new friend nor would I apologize for it. I said that Bunetta wanted to meet her and to be her friend, but she wouldn't give her a chance.

She replied that I could never understand what she had been through. Had I forgotten that she was beaten and raped by several men and thrown out on the street like a bag of garbage. Yet, I wanted her to brush all that aside and, just forget it. I wanted her to put on a happy face and be sociable to my new friend because that's what I expected from her.

"I told her how sorry I was and that I knew she had been through hell. I said that sometimes I wondered how she kept getting herself into these terrible situations.

"Then she screamed at me and accused me of believing everything that happened was her fault. This just kept getting better and better. Then she looked at me and said that she wanted to ask me something. Was it my fault that my parents ignored me all of my life? Was it my fault that her brother had ignored me all of these years? She implied that perhaps I had a character flaw that makes ignoring me easy?

"I said now Stella you're just being mean to me. I told her she never should have left with that young man by herself. It wasn't the proper thing to do. I told her I had no idea who she was with or where she had gone. It was my belief that a lady should never put herself in that kind of situation

She spat back that she wasn't a lady, and if I had paid any attention, I would already know that. She said I had determined that she put herself in that situation, thereby it was her fault. The matter was settled and it was time for me to get out of her room.

I told her that she didn't deserve that, no one did, and I was sorry if I made her feel that way. That wasn't my intention.

She said that maybe it wasn't my intention, but it was what I believed. She told me she wanted to be alone and asked me to leave her room.

I asked her to forgive me for hurting her it was not what I meant to do.

She just looked at me.

"I closed the door and went to my room. *Well, that didn't go as planned.* I felt terrible for hurting Stella. But if I was honest with myself, I did blame her. She was a tease and a flirt, and she did things that always had people's tongues wagging. No one could control her. She did as she pleased. I did a favor for all of them taking her out of their hair for a while. I shouldn't be held responsible for the trouble she got into. Now she had managed to ruin my day. I should never have gone into her room.

"Joshua came up to our room a couple of hours later to let me know that our company had arrived. It was his Aunt Helen and his Uncle Jacques from Rapides Parish. They were here for a couple of days. They were already the proud grandparents of six grandchildren. Aunt Helen was here to celebrate her brother's first grandchild. Never mind that it would be awhile before our baby was due to arrive.

"We spent the afternoon with our company on the front porch

shelling beans and drinking ice cold lemonade. The ladies had decided it was too warm to drink coffee. Lemonade sounded much more appealing. Aunt Helen had brought us a couple of bags of baby clothes from her own grandchildren.

She said that a baby could never have enough clothes because they don't wear them long enough to wear out.

I thanked her for her kindness and put the clothes in our bedroom.

Uncle Jacques asked when he was going to see that pretty little Stella, was she hiding?

Mrs. Vernice looked at me and said that Stella was not feeling well, and that she was hoping Stella would start feeling better by morning and have breakfast with us.

"After visiting for several hours, I went upstairs and went through the baby clothes that Aunt Helen had brought me. Somehow, holding these tiny baby outfits in my hand made the pregnancy much more real to me. An overwhelming feeling of sadness and despair washed over me. It was so strong that I dropped to my knees and cried.

"What if something happened to my baby? What would I do? My mother lost four babies before she finally had me. What if that happened to me? I was filled with so much fear, I could hardly breathe. How did my mother handle that loss over and over?

"I couldn't imagine how she felt losing one baby after another. Her life and her loss suddenly became so real to me that I began to understand what drove her to madness. Maybe I had been too hard on her. It suddenly occurred to me that unless you go through something yourself, you can't really understand how it feels.

"I finally put myself in Stella's shoes and, in my mind, went through each terrifying moment of her ordeal. It was so horrifying that I had to make myself go through every single minute of what she had told me. I was so sorry for trivializing what had happened to her and so ashamed of myself. I knew I had to go to her and apologize for being so callous and unfeeling.

"I tiptoed to Stella's room and knocked lightly on her door. I didn't hear anything so I let myself into her room and walked to her bedside. She was just lying there, silently, with big tears running down her cheeks. I lay next to her side and wrapped my arms around her, and I started crying too.

"Through my tears, I asked her to forgive me. I was so sorry for not understanding, for not being there for her. I promised her that I would do better. I would be here for her, and do whatever she needed. I told her that she was my sister, my family and I wouldn't leave her alone.

"She didn't say a word, but I felt her squeeze my hand. We both fell asleep with my arms wrapped around her.

Ms. Carine closed her eyes and laid her head in her hands. At that moment, the clock chimed six times, and I jumped up, startled.

I said, "I have to go, it's much later than I thought."

Ms. Carine said, "Yes, dear you go on home now. I'll see you next week."

When I got to the front door to leave, it occurred to me that there was no question anymore of whether or not I could be here every Saturday. We had an understanding between us.

I wonder where Rosa is. She usually watches me leave. Oh well, I didn't have time to look around. It was already dark outside. I jumped in my car and started it up. I was anxious to get home and type up what I had learned today. As I was making the turn from Ms. Carine's driveway to the road, I happened to look in the rear view mirror. In the distance, I could see the little girl walking toward the house. Behind her, there was another little girl following her. This girl was black and looked older than her and was dressed in what appeared to be a sack cloth dress. I watched both of them until they disappeared from my sight.

Just then I remembered the photo that I had shot of the bayou that morning on my way to Ms. Carine's house. I was anxious to have my film developed. The following Monday on my way to work, I stopped and dropped off my roll of film.

I picked it up that afternoon and tore open the package to go through my prints while still in my car. When I found the print, I could see a pirogue in the bayou with an old black man sitting in it, looking back at me. I almost jumped out of my seat. There was no one in that bayou yesterday morning, of that I was sure. *Who was he and where had he come from?* I wondered. Things kept getting stranger and stranger.

Things were a little strained between Justine and me at work. I wasn't happy with the fact that she had called my friends, telling them she was worried about me. I had quit sharing my stories with her because of it. I felt isolated because there was no one to talk to anymore. I needed to share the things that I was seeing and hearing with someone, but preferably, with someone who didn't think I was losing my mind.

Work was slow for a change, which gave Justine and me a chance to talk.

"Hey, look, I'm sorry about what I said to your friend Margaret," said Justine.

"Yeah, what was that about? I asked, "I thought you were interested in what I've been doing."

"I am interested. I love hearing about Ms. Carine's life. It's killing me not knowing what's been happening over there," said Justine.

"Then why did you tell Margaret that you were worried about me?" I said.

"She was the one who called because she was worried about you," said Justine. "She's worried about you spending so much time with this old woman that nobody around here knows. I'm just worried about your safety. I don't trust this woman, Rosa. I don't think she's a good person. I'm worried about this little girl that you keep seeing but can never get close enough to talk to. Now what about that ghost you saw in the bathroom? That would be it for me. But you keep going back there. I guess I just don't understand it."

"Of course, you don't understand it because I don't even understand it," I said. "I saw another ghost. She was standing in the corner of the bathroom, dripping water and blood. I was watching her in the mirror. As she was picking her head up to look at me, I turned around and she was gone."

"Oh my God, I can't believe you saw that, said Justine. Was it the same girl that you saw bleeding in the bathtub?" she asked.

"That's a good question. I'm not sure, I replied. She had her head down so I didn't see her face."

"Did you scream?" asked Justine.

"No, actually, I didn't scream. I couldn't breathe I was so afraid. I ran out of the room and ran right into Rosa.

"She came back into the bathroom with me and we checked the floor to see if it was wet with water or blood. Of course, it was dry. So Rosa scolded me as usual for seeing things that weren't there. She also made it clear, again, in case I had forgotten, that I was not to tell Ms. Carine what I had seen. In fact, I took what she said as a threat.

"I'm not sure if she's trying to protect Ms. Carine or if she's hiding things from her intentionally," I said. "Those two are tied at the hip. I guess what I'm trying to say is that Rosa has been with Ms. Carine since she's ten years old. It's only natural that she tries to protect her."

"Yes, I would agree with that," said Justine, "except for the fact that I get the impression that Rosa is jealous of your relationship with Ms. Carine. And jealous and insecure people can do strange and terrible things."

"So you're saying that I should be careful because there's no telling what Rosa may do to me?"

"Yes, dumbass, that's what I'm saying!" screamed Justine. "You just mentioned that she threatened you. What has to happen before you take her seriously? Is she going to have to hurt you first?"

"I think I will talk to Ms. Carine about Rosa and her attitude toward me," I replied. "Maybe I'll figure out what I'm doing to aggravate her and I can stop doing it. I need time to think about this."

The week at work went by much faster now that Justine and I were talking again. It's really hard to work side by side with someone that you're angry with. I was looking forward to this week's visit. I was amazed by the fact that Ms. Carine had been pregnant and wondering if she would lose the baby like her mother had. From what I could see, she had outlived all of her family and I knew that this part of her story wouldn't be easy for her to share.

I woke up Saturday morning to the windows rattling from the wind gusting. I hurried to the window to look outside to see what was going on. It was dark and gray outside and there were bursts of lightning strikes lighting up the sky. The wind was so strong that the trees seemed to move on their own accord. I turned on the news so I could see what was going on. There was another cold front coming in, with gusty winds and a possibility of hail.

I was afraid to drive in this weather but couldn't stand the thought of not going. I decided to wait for a couple of hours to see if the weather would clear. While waiting for the weather to calm down, I collected my thoughts. I needed to think things through before confiding in Ms. Carine the problem I was having with Rosa. I was afraid that Ms. Carine would scold her and then that would just intensify things between Rosa and me.

At about ten that morning, things seemed to quiet down a bit. The wind didn't seem to be blowing as hard. I bundled up and got on the road to Ms. Carine's house. I slowed down on the bridge over the bayou and watched the wind blowing in the trees. I looked around to see if there was anyone paddling around in the bayou, but there wasn't a soul in sight.

When I turned into her driveway, I realized how bare and desolate this place looked in the dead of winter. This year was by far the coldest winter I could remember since I was a little girl.

When I got to her house, I could see the smoke from the fireplace in the library and the formal living room. The house looked cozy, and I was anxious to get in out of this bitterly cold weather. Rosa opened the door and took my coat.

She said, "Ms. Carine is waiting for you in the formal living room. You're late."

I replied, "Yes, I know I'm late. I was waiting for the wind to subside before driving here."

She gave me a look that said, aren't you the sassy one today?

I ignored her and walked right past her.

I apologized to Ms. Carine for being late.

She was understanding and said, "I'm so glad you waited. That wind is too strong to be driving in."

I made myself comfortable in the old rocker, and Ms. Carine had Rosa bring us each a steaming cup of chocolate milk.

"Now, where were we?" Ms. Carine asked.

"You were in bed with Stella, comforting her," I replied.

"I'm glad you're paying attention," laughed Ms. Carine.

She resumed her story.

"I woke up early the next morning. The sun was just rising. At first, I was confused. I wasn't sure where I was. Then I saw Stella's beautiful long curls covering her shoulders. The sun was peeking through the curtains and falling on her hair. From where I was laying, her hair looked like the sun setting on waves in the ocean.

"Oh, if only we were as good and as righteous as we believed ourselves to be. Our world is only as big as the people we surround ourselves with, I thought. And if we cannot have empathy for those we profess to love, then what kind of world are we living in? I professed then and there to open my heart to Stella and to try harder to understand her pain. I vowed to stop judging her and to be there for her if she needed me

"I quietly got up and went to my room. Joshua was in bed but he wasn't asleep. He took my hand and pulled me next to him. He held me without speaking, and we both fell back asleep. We awoke an hour later with Lydia knocking lightly on our door.

"She said that breakfast was ready and everyone was already at the table."

Joshua told her that we would be there shortly.

He quickly got dressed to go downstairs, looked at me and asked if I would be long.

" I told him I would only be a few minutes, but for him to go ahead and start without me. I wanted to try to get Stella to come downstairs with me."

I knocked lightly on Stella's door and I heard a low voice say come in. To my surprise, she was already dressed in an elegant, stunning lavender satin dress.

I asked her if she felt well enough to come down for breakfast.

"She replied that she did and that she wouldn't miss seeing her Aunt Helen and Uncle Jacque, and that she would be down in a minute.

I replied, "You look absolutely beautiful in that dress, but aren't you overdressed for breakfast?"

To that she remarked, how she dressed was none of my business, she already had a mother, she didn't need another one."

"I closed her door, surprised and offended by her remark. Well, so much for the sympathy and guilt I had been feeling. I wasn't sure what was going through Stella's mind right now. With her, you could never be quite sure. I felt my guard go up again. I would never understand what drove that girl.

"I went down for breakfast, and I could tell Mrs. Vernice was aggravated with me for keeping all of them waiting. A few minutes later, Stella made her entrance into the dining room. She looked like a queen in that beautiful dress, and the way her family doted on her, she could have been. Her Uncle Jacque's face lit up when he saw her, and he hugged her, just a little too long from the look on Aunt Helen's face.

"Stella seemed to be back to her normal, flirtatious self. She had all the men eating out of her hand and the women loathing her. After breakfast, we retired to the front porch for coffee. Stella entertained everyone with stories of our trip to Boston. She made the people sound stupid and the food, unseasoned and bland. She kept looking at me out the corner of her eye to see how I was reacting to her stories about my home. She knew I didn't like confrontation, and she was doing her best to get me involved. Aunt Helen was staring at me, embarrassed by the things Stella was saying and not knowing what to do.

"I excused myself and walked to the bayou. I was so angry with Stella, I didn't know what to do. Just when I was feeling sympathy for her, she had to show her spiteful and mean side. A few minutes later, Joshua showed up to meet me at the bayou.

He told me not to pay any mind to Stella. He said that she was still angry at me for abandoning her on that train ride back. He said that she was jealous of my new friend. He reminded me of how Stella needed all of the attention focused on her, and she knew the only reason we had company was because I was pregnant with his baby."

CHAPTER EIGHT

"THE DEMISE OF STELLA"

I told him that I didn't know why Stella was the way she is, and I didn't really care anymore. I was tired of her drama, and I was tired of trying to be her friend. She was his sister and he could deal with her from now on. I said that I had a baby coming and that's what I was going to concentrate on."

"I spent the rest of that week working with my flowers and reading. I wrote a letter to Bunetta, and I anxiously awaited her response. The days and months flew by, and my belly kept growing. I could feel the baby kicking now. Joshua was having a crib built, and his mother had been knitting baby blankets and booties.

"After our company left, Stella again withdrew into her room. She stayed in her bedroom most days and avoided all of us. She took her meals in her room and turned everyone away from her door. When I did see her, she was always wrapped up in a big robe. I thought that was odd but had given up trying to figure her out.

"Stella was up to her old ways again leaving the house late in the afternoon and coming home later in the evening. I didn't have to share the bathroom with anyone anymore so I never met up with Stella. She was a mystery to me. I could tell that Mrs. Vernice was worried about Stella, but she would never admit that to me. I asked

Joshua if he had spoken to his sister lately, and he just shrugged his shoulders.

"We had been home about six months when I received a letter from Nadine. She hoped this letter would find Joshua and I in good health. She was writing to let me know that my Mother was quite ill and had taken to her bed. She was in good hands with Bertha and Nadine checked on her daily. My Mother was a woman with many regrets and pain in her heart. She wanted me to know that she had done the best she could with what she had. She asked for my forgiveness but she understood if I couldn't forgive her. Nadine asked me to be swift with my reply. She didn't believe that my Mother had long on this earth. She knew that my Mother had no right to ask me for forgiveness, but for my sake, she hoped that I would. She said by forgiving my mother it would free me in more ways than I could imagine. She inquired as to ow Stella was doing and she kept her in her prayers nightly. The chief had not found these men and the trail had gone cold. It appalled her to think that those men had gotten away with this horrendous crime.

"I read her letter over and over. Now that my Mother is dying, she wants my forgiveness. Why would I be surprised?

"I didn't feel like I could forgive her, but I would tell her that I did. I figured as the years went by, maybe I would forgive her. I just couldn't torment myself any longer wondering why my mother was the way she was. So I sat down and wrote Nadine a letter.

I asked Nadine to tell my mother that I forgave her. I would never understand why she withheld her love and attention from me all of my life. I would no longer try to figure her out or judge her. She is what life had made of her. I told her that I was expecting a baby in September and to please let my Mother know that she would be a grandmother. This was the reason that I couldn't make the trip to see her at this time. My prayer was for her to get well and live to meet her grandchild.

I asked Nadine to keep me informed of my mother's condition, and that I appreciated all that she did.

. . .

"I felt better telling my mother that I had forgiven her. But it didn't feel like I had. My Christian faith had taught me that I must forgive others as Christ had forgiven me. It taught me that forgiveness wasn't an emotion. It was an act of will. I hadn't forgotten the lessons that I had learned as a little girl sitting in that church alone. Every child attending church was sitting there with their parents except me. I felt so alone, so little. I kept going back week after week just to hear the priest proclaim God's love for his congregation. I needed to know that someone loved me, because I surely didn't feel loved at home.

"Thinking about that made me realize that I had already forgotten my desire to stop judging Stella and to be there for her in her pain. I went to her room and knocked lightly on her door. She didn't answer, so I tried to open the door. It was locked.

I said, "Stella it's me. Are you okay? Please say something, or I will go and get your father."

I heard her take a deep breath and then she told me to stop being so dramatic, that she was fine and what did I want?"

"I told her I just wanted to visit, because I hadn't spoken to her in months. I asked her why didn't she ever come out of her bedroom?

"She said she needed her privacy and had other reasons for staying in her room, and I would find out soon enough.

"I told her that didn't make any sense to me. She would soon welcome a new niece or nephew. I wanted her to see how huge my belly had gotten, and I wanted her to feel the baby kicking. I begged her to come out of her room or to let me in.

"She replied that she couldn't do that, but she was very happy for me and Joshua. She said we should love and protect this child and shower it with our love. Then she asked if they had caught the men that hurt her.

"I told her that they hadn't caught those men yet. I assured her that they were still looking, and they would catch them, even though I knew it was a lie.

I knew they were at a dead end on this case, but I wanted to give her some hope.

"She said for me to keep telling myself that lie, and maybe one day I would believe it. She for one knew better than to wait for that to happen. She was just curious to know if I had heard anything."

"I told her that if I heard anything she would be the first one to know.

"She mocked me and said she would have to believe me, because I was so righteous and just.

"I asked her why she was so mean to me when I was just trying to reach out to her.

"She said she didn't know why, I just brought out the worst in her. She stated that I had told her about the hard life I had as a child. Yet I was still so naive and at the same time, proud. She guessed she just didn't understand me or my type.

"Well, that makes two of us then, because I do not understand you at all," I said to her.

You are trying to understand something you never will, she said.

I kept quiet for a moment and then I said, "If I ask you something, will you answer me?

"Ask away, she said.

" I've often wondered where you go when you take off in the fields and don't come back for hours.

"She said that she would go to meet her best friend in the world.

"I stated that I wasn't aware she had a best friend and why hadn't she told me about her?"

"She asked me why I assumed her best friend was a girl because she assured me that was not the case. She stated that he and she were the same age, born at the same time, on the same day. But they lived worlds apart.

"I was so confused," said Carine. "How can they live worlds apart and be best friends?"

"She then confided what she had been hiding all of this time. She said it's because I am white, and he is black. She then went on to tell me that both of them were born on this cotton plantation on the same day. They both came into this world, seconds apart. She was rich, and he was poor. She lived in a beautiful home with all the food she could ever eat. He lived in a shack and went hungry lots of nights. They had grown up together on this plantation in two different worlds. She said the crazy thing was it was her that was jealous of him. She said she had been so lonely her entire life.

Her mother had no time for her. She paid others to raise her child. The only thing she ever wanted from Stella was for her to get out of her hair and leave her alone. She said her mother had done things to her, things I could never imagine.

But on the other hand, Edie had a wonderful and loving mother. She had ten children and was tender and loving toward all of them. She had been a mother to her too. She spent most of her young life in that shack trying to be a part of their family. As she grew older, she realized that they had to put up with her. They had no other choice. She said she was sure they wondered why this rich little white girl never wanted to go home. She said she now knows that when she was at their house, they had to watch what they said in front of her. In case she went back to the big house and repeated what they said. She acknowledged now how hard that must have been on all of them.

She said it was an embarrassment for her mother to know that she was spending time at the slave quarters. She didn't want anyone to know so she just ignored it and didn't talk about it. Stella taught Edie everything that she learned at school. He didn't get to go to school much. He had to work in the fields. As they got older Edie's mother tried to discourage her from spending time with him.

She told Stella that it wasn't right, that people would talk. Stella didn't care what she thought or for that matter what anyone thought. Edie was the only person who truly knew and understood her. She could tell him anything, and he listened without judging her.

Stella asked me if I knew how rare that was, to not be judged.

It started while they were teenagers, they kissed and started fooling around. They didn't realize the danger they were putting themselves in. Once they started, they couldn't stop. They were burning up for one another. It went on for months, until his mother found them in their secret spot near the swamps. His mother forbid Stella to go anywhere close to Edie or she would tell her mother, and Edie's father beat him until he was unrecognizable. It was the only way Edie's father could make him understand the severity of what they had done and the danger of anyone else finding out would result in Edie's death.

A couple of months went by without her having her period. Her breasts were tender, and she was nauseated every day. She knew she was in deep trouble, and she didn't know what to do. She went and found Edie's mom and let her know because she couldn't go to anyone else. Edie's mother got a potion for her to drink, and she got so sick that she thought she was going to die. The potion worked. She passed the baby hours later. Their baby is buried under that old tree in the swamps. That's where she spends many of her days, keeping him company.

"She wanted to know if I was happy now that I knew her secret and was my curiosity satisfied?

"I just sat there on the floor in front of her door in shock. I didn't know what to say. I was disgusted by her and at the same time, I felt sorry for her. I just sat in silence, I couldn't think of anything to say to her," said Carine.

Laughing she said she had finally found a way to shut me up.

Shaking my head, I got up, and started to walk back to my room.

I told her that I needed some time to digest everything she had just told me.

"She told me to go away, and leave her alone. She said for me to go and bury my head in the sand. It's what I was best at, in case I hadn't figured that out yet.

"I told her she wasn't playing fair and that she couldn't expect me to just accept all that she had just shared with me."

She said that she didn't expect anything from me, she never has, and she never would. She was a big girl and she could take care of herself. She had been doing it all of her life. I needed to go to my room, to my little life and let her be. She begged me to stay away from her and leave her alone.

Sighing deeply I said to her that I had only one more question to ask. I wanted to know if Joshua was aware of what she had been through.

She replied that there were no secrets between she and her brother, the only secrets that stood were between Joshua and myself.

What secret is Joshua hiding from me, I asked, you must tell me!

Stella remained silent.

"I'm trying desperately to understand I said to her. I just need some time to think about what you've told me.

She said for me to take all the time I needed.

"I went to my room, took a hot bath, and crawled into bed. I was in shock at the things my sister-in-law had shared with me and I fell into a deep sleep.

"At some point in the night, I thought I saw Stella at the side of my bed, watching me sleep. I woke up, and no one was there. I knew it was a dream because she was big and pregnant just like me.

"In the morning, I was startled awake by a horrific piercing scream that went on and on. I jumped out of bed and ran out of my room. The scream was coming from downstairs. When I got to the bottom of the stairs, I saw that it was Lydia who was screaming. At that moment, everyone in the house was up and trying to get downstairs. Lydia was standing at the bathroom door. When she saw me, she said, "Oh no, Ms. Carine, you mustn't go in there." I shrugged her hand off my shoulder and entered the bathroom.

"Stella was lying in the bathtub filled with water and blood. She had given birth to a perfect little boy, then slit her wrists. Her beautiful red curls were floating on the water, her beautiful face serene. It is a scene that has burned itself into my subconscious. Falling hard to my knees, I began screaming. I don't remember who picked me up off of the floor. It was the first time in my life that I can remember myself fainting.

Ms. Carine looked at me with tears glistening in her eyes and said, "Danielle, that's enough for today."

I looked at her and shook my head yes. I squeezed her hand and without saying a word, I left.

So it was Stella I had seen in the bathroom. Her presence haunts that room, and with good cause.

Now that I finally knew what happened to her, I wondered if I would see her again. I couldn't wait to get home and put all of this on paper. Today was a major breakthrough for me. Discovering what happened to Stella was momentous. Our visits and the sharing of her life story were taking a toll on Ms. Carine's health. I dreaded seeing her go through those painful memories.

These memories took her back in time to live through these unpleasant and painful events that she would rather not think about. But she was determined to share this with me. She wanted her story told. I did still want to see a picture of Stella. I had only seen her in death. I wanted to remember her pretty face while she was young and beautiful.

At work, I shared my story with Justine. She was mesmerized with Stella's story and everything that had happened to her. We spent every minute we could that day talking about it. I had such a burden on my heart for Ms. Carine, I would pray for her. That was the one thing I could do. I spent the rest of the week tweaking my story by adding details that I had forgotten.

Saturday was here before I knew it. I woke up to a cold and rainy day. It was a stay in my pajamas kind of day. But I bundled up and, at the last minute, grabbed my camera. Stella was dead but this story was far from over.

When I got to the bridge over the bayou, the rain came pouring down. How fitting, I thought, tears from heaven. I felt very solemn this morning and hoped that Ms. Carine could finish her story.

When I got to her house, the door opened and I saw Ms. Carine standing there, waving at me. I ran to the house in the pouring rain and pulled my rubber boots off on the porch. She met me at the door with hot chocolate and a towel.

"I wouldn't have blamed you for not coming out in this horrible weather," said Ms. Carine.

"I would have to be deathly ill to not show up," I said as I laughed. "I'm anxious to hear the rest of the story. I've been thinking about it all week."

"Well then, let's make ourselves comfortable and I'll get started," said Ms. Carine. She resumed her tale as soon as we were settled.

"When I awoke after fainting, I was in excruciating pain. Mrs. Vernice was the first person I saw hovering over me. Her face was pale and clammy, and her hands were shaking. I cried out, 'Stella,' and she put her hand over my mouth. She told me I was in labor, I needed to save my strength, and that Joshua had gone for the doctor.

"The pain in my stomach was unbearable and I cried out. Mrs.Vernice put a cool washcloth on my head and assured me that everything would be okay.

"I couldn't imagine how she could help me after finding her daughter and grandson dead just minutes ago. She was in shock. We all were, but babies don't wait and this one was coming fast.

CHAPTER NINE

"THE BIRTH"

"A few minutes later, Joshua walked in with Doctor Dupre. Joshua picked me up and carried me to our bedroom. He laid me on the bed where I would give birth. Lydia came in and helped me undress into a nightgown. The labor pains were excruciating and exhausting. I spent hours thrashing on the bed sure that my body would soon split in two. I finally fell asleep for a little while. When I woke up, I turned over and noticed an envelope sticking out of the book on my nightstand. My name was on it, and I recognized it as Stella's handwriting. My hands were shaking so bad that I had trouble opening the envelope. Her note to me said,

"When you find this you will know, I am no more."

She said she was no longer in anguish, and no longer in pain, nor did she feel any fear. She said that she chose to live the life she lived and that she also chose the way she would die. She told me not to mourn for her. She again affirmed that she had chosen to end her life this way. Her one request was that I bury her and her baby next to his brother, near the swamp beneath the old oak tree.

She signed it, your sister.

"I knew then that she had been in my room last night, it wasn't a dream. Why hadn't she awakened me? There could only be one explanation: she had planned this. She was waiting to go into labor, give birth then take her baby's life away. She would murder her baby. He wasn't baptized, and she had committed the ultimate sin of suicide. She would surely burn in hell.

"Why would anyone choose that? Did she think she was punishing those men for what they did to her? All these months she hid her pregnancy from us, waiting for that perfect moment.

"I didn't want to believe this. I couldn't believe her capable of such a thing. She was headstrong, but she wasn't crazy. Or was she? I thought I knew her so well, but apparently I didn't know her at all.

"Now I started to wonder about Joshua and the secret he was hiding from me. What was it? Did I even want to know? Because once you know something you can't go back to not knowing. You have to deal with it or it will drive you mad. If Stella had taught me anything, she had taught me that.

"Stella's secrets were so much worse than I could have imagined. She knew what Joshua was hiding from me, but she took that secret to her grave. They both knew each other's secrets and would never betray one another. Blood was thicker than water, or so I've been told. But I couldn't think about that right now. My baby was coming.

"I stayed in labor for twelve hours. I believed that I was dying, and that I would never see my baby. But finally, the pain was over. I had a baby girl. She was perfect in every way. Her skin was pink and her hair was the color of the sun. She had two perfect dimples in both of her chubby cheeks. I took one look at that angelic face and immediately named her Isabella Renee` Dubois. The doctor spanked her little buttocks, and she let out a gloriously loud, healthy scream.

"It was then and only then that I felt myself really start to relax, and I finally got some sleep. I slept soundly without dreaming until Joshua woke me to let our baby nurse. I couldn't wait to hold my darling daughter in my arms and truly did not know what love was until that moment.

"Unbeknownst to me, while I was in labor, the family had buried

Stella and her son in the family plot behind the house. At that time, the church wouldn't bury someone who had committed suicide on hallowed ground. It was believed at that time you suffered eternal damnation and went straight to hell if you took your own life. Those people were buried outside of the church's burial grounds. But Joshua's family had a private family cemetery on their land, and Stella and the baby were buried there.

"The sheriff had investigated, and her death was ruled a suicide. Nothing was said of the baby she had delivered. I tried to talk to Joshua about Stella, but he refused to listen. I showed him the note she had left me. He read it, threw it on floor, and rushed out of the room.

"A few hours later, he returned and ordered me to never show that note to anyone else. He said that no one must ever read it. Did I understand?"

"I couldn't look him in the eye so I just hung my head and nodded yes.

"Joshua took me by the shoulders, gripping them hard, and asked me to promise him that I would destroy the note and never tell another soul what she had written.

"I told him he was hurting me and then I promised him.

"He left the room, and Rosa came in to help me with Isabella. Rosa slept on the floor next to me and helped me tend to the baby. Thankfully, Isabella was a good baby and I got plenty of rest. I think Joshua was disappointed that we had a girl. He had his heart set on a boy.

"It's hard to explain to you the range of emotions that everyone was feeling the week that Isabella was born. To lose Stella in the way that we lost her was heartbreaking. To find out that she was also pregnant and had managed to hide it from us was crazy. All of us were in shock finding her that morning. Then for me to go straight into childbirth was overwhelming. To lose someone you love is the hardest thing in the world to accept.

It takes time to even accept that they are gone. There are many stages of grief, and I feel like I went through all of them in one week. "Throughout all of this sadness, there was nothing and no one who could steal this joy from my heart. I finally had a child that was a part of me, someone to love unconditionally. I had someone and something to live for.

"I believe that Isabella helped Mrs. Vernice get through these dark days. She came upstairs every afternoon and took Isabella for a couple of hours.

"She would sit on the porch in her old rocking chair and rock that baby for hours on end. One afternoon, I decided to go and keep her company. When I opened the door to go out on the porch, I heard Mrs. Vernice softly crying. She was holding Isabella on her chest and as she rocked the baby, her tears fell. I backed away quietly so as not to disturb her and went back upstairs. I realized that this was a healing process for her. Our little girl was already helping to heal and mend our broken hearts.

"Joshua was not as attentive a father as I would have liked. I don't know what I expected from him. He hadn't been attentive to me as my husband. Why did I expect him to be a doting father to our child?

"But where I accepted less than I deserved for myself, I would not accept anything but the best for my daughter. I was determined that she would have the best of everything. She would have everything that I had done without. As long as there was breath in my body, I would make sure of that.

"When Isabella was a couple of months old and I was feeling better, I decided to ride to the edge of the swamp. I was looking for Stella's tree. I wanted to put flowers on her baby boy's grave. I couldn't fulfill her request to be buried there and that bothered me, so putting flowers on his grave was the least I could do. The only time I had ever been to the swamp was with Stella and that was years ago when I first came to Louisiana. She had taken me to see her favorite spot. A spot where she had told me was a good place to get rid of a body. When I thought back on that conversation, it gave me chills all over. I never in my entire life could have guessed the secrets that Stella held in her heart. Before she turned sixteen years old, she had already aborted and buried a baby.

"I was beginning to understand why she was so cynical at such a young age. She had already been through so much before I ever met her. I thought I had such a rough life growing up. At this moment, I was rethinking that.

"I was afraid that I would get lost in the swamp. All of the trees looked alike. I was so worried that I would come across an alligator or a water moccasin that I found myself turned around, not sure of where I was.

"I wondered around in the swamp for hours, panicking and screaming for help. In the distance, I could see someone walking towards me. I started running toward him, screaming at the top of my lungs. I tripped over an old stump and fell on my hands. A snake, just inches away from my face, slithered past me into the murky water. I felt a flash of pain in my side. I looked down and realized that I had fallen into a patch of thorns. I started crying sure that I would die here and never see my baby again. Then I heard a voice say, 'Ms. Carine, are you all right?'

"I looked up and saw that it was a young black man. I had never seen him before, but he knew who I was and I could see the concern In his eyes for me.

"I told him that I had fallen into a patch of thorns.

"He told me to stay still there was no need to worry, he would get me out of there.

"He had a pocket knife on him, and he started cutting away at the branch at my side. He spoke softly the whole time he worked on freeing me.

He stated how dangerous the swamp could be and how easy it was to get lost in it. After getting me out of there safely, he walked me back to my horse. He wanted to know what I was doing out there in the first place, all by myself.

"I told him I was looking for Stella's tree, and he froze. It was in that moment that I figured out this must be Edie.

I asked him to bring me to her tree.

"He looked at me out of the corner of his eyes and nodded. He helped me get on my horse then slowly walked me there. It took a while to find it. I had wandered quite far from where I was originally.

"He pointed to the old oak tree then he walked away, giving me privacy. The tree was huge with branches sweeping to the ground, making an enclosure. Curly gray moss hung from the branches, giving it a majestic feel. The grass had been cut recently, and there were two comfortable logs under it for sitting. To my astonishment, under the tree there was an old iron cross. There were flowers planted all around it, marking the grave of that poor, sweet, innocent baby.

"I sat on one of the logs and from this location I had a perfect view of the swamp and the ancient cypress trees surrounding it. I realized at that moment it wasn't only Stella's secret place. Edie knew about it and was a regular visitor. He had been taking care of their baby too.

"He must have loved Stella, but he had enough common sense to know it could never happen, not in their lifetime, and not if he wanted to live.

"I sat for a while then returned to my horse. Edie was still there, waiting to walk my horse out. I thanked him again for helping me, and he said it wasn't a good idea for me to come out here again. He warned me of the people who had wandered into the swamp, never to be seen again.

"I asked him if he went there often to check on his baby.

In disbelief he looked at me and said he couldn't believe she had told me. It was their secret and she had sworn to take this secret to her grave.

" I said that considering she took another baby to the grave with her, I supposed she wanted someone here to take care of the one she left behind.

"Edie was angry and said that he had been and would continue caring for his baby.

"I asked Edie if he had been caring for him while Stella was alive.

"He told me that both he and Stella were responsible for this life being taken. He stated that he would continue to come to this old tree and make sure that their baby boy would never be forgotten. He said there was no reason for me to return here. He didn't know about Stella's note and her asking me to bury her and her baby under this old tree next to her firstborn and I couldn't tell him. I couldn't honor that request because she and her baby had already been buried while I was in labor.

"I told him he didn't have to worry because I wouldn't be back. I got on my horse and headed back home. I turned around and asked Edie one more question.

"I asked him if he loved Stella.

"He told me that he loved her more than anything. They were a part of each other even though they came from different worlds. They were playmates and best friends and when they got older, their love changed to something else, something bigger. It was bigger than both of them. He tried to back away from her, but Stella wouldn't hear of it and she always got her way, no matter what the consequences.

"I looked at Edie and knew that what he had just said was the truth. Anyone that knew Stella realized that about her right away. I agreed with him and turned my horse toward home.

"When I got home, Mrs.Vernice was on the porch waiting for me. She asked me where had I been and what had happened to me.

"I told her that I rode toward the swamp and got lost. I didn't offer her any other explanation. I went up to my room and took a long bath. I couldn't get Stella out of my mind. I just wanted to spend the evening holding my baby girl close to me. When Stella said it was a good place to hide a body, she was speaking from experience. She was hiding a body, her own baby's. I had felt uneasy about her dying request. She had placed on my shoulders a task I was not capable of doing. Leave it to Stella to leave me in turmoil even in her death.

"It was so hard for me to grasp her situation. I was beginning to understand why she had been so cold and callous. She had done and seen things I never could have imagined.

"I had no plans to visit her secret place in the swamp ever again. I would let Edie take care of his baby and let him make atonement for both of their sins. As for burying her and her baby under that tree, that was a request I could not fulfill.

With that, Ms. Carine leaned her head against the old rocker and closed her eyes.

I said, "Ms. Carine, it's late and you're tired. I'm going to go home now. I'll see you next week."

She smiled at me and said in a voice that trembled, "Yes, I feel extremely exhausted right now."

I said, "I'll make my way out, you get some rest."

Rosa met me in the hall and gave me my purse. She said, "These memories are very hard on Ms. Carine. She is reliving parts of her life better left forgotten."

I said, "Yes, I understand, but it's important to her to have her story told."

"Yes, I know that," said Rosa. "I couldn't stop her if I tried. And believe me, I have tried."

I opened the door and walked out onto the porch. There, at the end of the porch, was the little girl kneeling in the grass, her back against the house. I started walking slowly to her so as not to frighten her away.

I said, "Hello, my name is Danielle. What's yours?"

She didn't answer me and she had the saddest look on her sweet little face. She got up and started walking away from me.

I said, "Please don't leave, I just want to talk to you."

She kept walking toward the back yard, so I kept following her. It started raining again and my shoes were soaking wet as I sloshed through the mud soaked grass. Dammit! I had left my boots on Ms. Carine's porch.

"Do you live around here?" I asked. "Can you please tell me your name?"

She pointed towards the house then she started running toward the pond in the back yard.

At that moment, Rosa opened the back door and hollered at me, "Ms. Danielle what are you doing?"

I turned around and said, "Rosa, I'm talking to the little girl. Here she is."

I turned back, and she was gone.

"Didn't you see her too?" I asked.

"There is no one there, Ms. Danielle. Get out of that rain before you catch your death of cold," said Rosa.

"She was here. She was in front of the porch. I followed her to the back yard and asked her where she lived, and she pointed to this house. Could you please explain why she pointed to this house?"

"I can't explain nothing to you," said Rosa. "I can tell you for sure that there is no little girl living here with us."

"Well, did you at least see her this time?" I asked in a pleading voice.

"No ma'am, I didn't see no one out there but you sloshing in the mud," said Rosa.

"Okay," I said. "I'm going to get in my car and go home right now. It doesn't matter if you believe me or not. That was the closest I've been to her yet. She's starting to trust me and I'm not giving up on her. I will get to the bottom of this and I will find out who she is and where she lives."

"You do that," said Rosa. "But now you need to get on home and get out of those wet clothes and shoes before you catch pneumonia."

I had to take my wet muddy shoes off before I got in my car. I was soaked to the bone and aggravated beyond belief. Rosa infuriated me and made me doubt my sanity. This was the closest I had gotten to the little girl. She was a beautiful child underneath all that dirt.

The dress she was wearing looked homemade. It had once been white and had a bow tied at her waist. She was always barefoot and dirty. Her hair was shoulder length, wavy and blonde. Her eyes were a very rare and beautiful emerald green.

I got home, stripped down, and took a long, hot shower. I couldn't wait to write everything down. I wrote until midnight and made myself go to bed to get some sleep so I could clean house tomorrow and get ready for work the next day.

"Justine's eyes were bright with excitement when I got to work the next day. We made ourselves a cup of coffee and sat down for a few minutes to visit before the telephone starting ringing. I told her about the birth of Isabella and the death of Stella. I repeated word for word the suicide note Stella had left in Carine's bedroom. I shared the story of the swamp and Edie and the baby buried under the old oak tree. I finished with the encounter I had with the little girl and how she pointed to Ms. Carine's house as her home, when asked where she lived. Repeating the story to Justine helped me put things in perspective. It made Ms. Carine's story clearer in my mind.

Justine was shocked by Stella's secret life and secret love. "Never in a million years," she said, would I have guessed what she was hiding. To fall in love with a slave boy and have to abort their baby is unbelievable," said Justine. Then to bury that baby and spend her days alone at his grave was sad beyond belief. All of those years and she couldn't dare speak of it or share it with anyone. That was enough to drive her crazy."

"Tell me about the little girl," she added.

"When I walked out of Ms. Carine's house, she was crouched against the house at the end of the porch, sitting in the rain. She started walking around the house, and I think she wanted me to follow her. The wind was blowing, and the rain was falling hard. It didn't seem to bother her at all. I had a coat and shoes on, and I was shivering with cold. She was barefoot, with a short sleeve dress on and not shivering at all."

"How old do you think the little girl is?" asked Justine.

"I'm not sure how old she is, but I would guess at least six or seven," I replied.

"What did she look like?" asked Justine.

"She is a beautiful child underneath all that dirt," I said. "She has an olive complexion with shoulder length, honey-colored blonde hair. Her eyes are a deep emerald green, which mesmerized me. She has full, light pink lips much too sensual for a child that young. I've never seen her smile she always looks so serious."

"Why would she point to Ms. Carine's house when you asked her where she lived?" asked Justine.

"I'm not sure," I said. Could she be living under their house without them knowing it?"

"That would be insane, said Justine, "How could she survive?"

"I don't know, but she's always in the same old dirty white dress, and she's always barefoot."

"Maybe she's one of those feral kids, being raised by animals. It doesn't make any sense," said Justine.

"What doesn't make sense is that both Rosa and Ms. Carine have never seen her, or so they say," I replied.

"What a mystery this is!" said Justine. "Ask Ms. Carine again to show you a picture of Stella. Ask her what happened to her daughter too."

"I have to wait for her to get to that part of the story," I said to Justine. "She just shared with me that she had a baby. I have to give her time to tell me Isabella's story. This isn't easy for her. She relives these memories, and it opens up old wounds."

"Where does this little girl fit in?" asked Justine.

"I'm not sure, but I did see her the very first time I went to Ms. Carine's house. She was in the upstairs bedroom looking out of the window at me."

"Have you noticed any pictures of anyone in her home?" asked Justine.

"That's a good question, Justine. I haven't seen any except for the big painting of herself over the mantel in the formal living room."

"That's strange in itself, don't you think?" said Justine.

"Yes, it is a little strange," I replied. "I guess I will check out her bookshelves when I'm there."

"I find it weird that you haven't already looked around, said Justine. Why is that?"

"It's really strange, but when I get there we generally sit before the fire and we don't move. Her life is fascinating, and before I know it, we have been sitting for hours.

"How is the house decorated?" asked Justine. You must have noticed that."

"There is a lot of fancy woodwork everywhere, I said. Over each window and each door are beautiful carved moldings. Even the baseboards have carved moldings over them."

"So you have noticed some things in there," said Justine.

"Yes, there are paintings on some of the walls," I said, struggling to remember. There is a small painting of pink roses in a vase on a nightstand next to Ms. Carine's bed."

Who painted it?" asked Justine.

"That's a good question too," I said. "I really don't know who painted any of them."

"That's a good place to start, said Justine.When you go this weekend, make a point of looking at them to see if there is a signature. She may have a fortune hanging on her walls. How cool would that be!"

"That's a good idea. She shouldn't mind me asking since they are hanging up for anyone to see. I will also ask her again about Stella's picture."

"What about mirrors? Does she have any huge, elaborate ones hanging up?" asked Justine.

"There is a large one in the dining room. The only other mirror I've seen is the one over the sink in the bathroom," I replied and I'm afraid to look in that one. She does have a beautiful chandelier in the entryway."

"So you have been looking around," said Justine. "It would have been weird if you hadn't."

"Why do you say that?" I asked.

"Because I know you, Danielle, and you're nosy that way," laughed Justine.

I laughed and said, "What can I say? You know me too well and you're absolutely right but I prefer to believe that I'm a decorator at heart!

When I got home from work, I thought about my conversation with Justine. She was right. My nature was to inspect anyone's house when I visited there. The first thing I looked for were framed photographs around the house. Second on my list would be decorative items scattered throughout the house. At the same time I was examining these things, I would be admiring the woodwork and floors.

The week dragged by, and I spent my time writing down the things Ms. Carine had told me. I tried to find out more information about Ms. Carine's family at the library, but I wasn't having much luck.

I woke up early Saturday morning to a beautiful sunny day but still so cold outside. I picked up biscuits and sausage for breakfast and headed to her house. When I got to the bridge I pulled over to get a few shots of the bayou.

CHAPTER TEN

"EXPLORING"

To my surprise there were two old colored men sitting on the side of the bayou fishing. They were dressed in raggedy clothes and wore straw hats on their heads. They were fishing with cane poles, just like in the old days. *Where would you even find a hat like that these days?* I started waving my arms and yelling hello, but they were oblivious to me. It was as if they couldn't see me. I got back in my car after taking a few pictures of them. I had an urgent need to prove to myself that they were really there.

I got to Ms. Carine's house and scanned the area for the little girl. She was nowhere to be seen. Smoke was pouring up the chimney from the fireplace in the library. I suppose today's storytelling would take place in that room. That was okay with me. It would give me a chance to check out the bookshelves.

Rosa answered the door and said for me to go into the kitchen for breakfast.

I told her that I had picked up biscuits for breakfast.

"Well, if I could read your mind, I wouldn't have troubled myself to cook this morning," said Rosa.

"I'm sorry, I replied. I should have let you know."

Rosa just shot me a dirty look and took the bag from my hands.

There was no way to please this woman. I walked in the kitchen, and Ms. Carine was sitting at the table looking out the back window.

"Good morning," Ms. Carine, I said in a cheerful voice.

"Well, someone is in an extraordinary good mood today!" exclaimed Ms. Carine. Come in, Danielle, and sit with me. We will have our breakfast. Tell me what has happened for you to have such a big smile on your face this morning."

"Nothing in particular has happened, I replied. I woke up to a beautiful, sunny day, and I'm just grateful to be healthy and alive."

"You should be grateful every day for this gift of life," said Ms. Carine, as she looked deeply into my eyes. "Even the cold, dark, dreary days have a place in your life. Everything that happens to you happens for a reason, she said quietly. The problem is that most people don't put it together until the end of their lives. Because of that, they don't see how the pieces fit together like a puzzle. Pay attention to your life, Danielle. We all have a number of days to live, and not one of us knows what our number will be."

At that moment, Rosa came to the table with bacon, eggs, and biscuits. She poured us each a hot, steaming cup of coffee to drink with our breakfast. She left my bag of biscuits on the counter. I didn't say anything. Her biscuits were so much better than the ones I had picked up.

When breakfast was over, we went into the library. Instead of sitting in the rocker as I normally did, I walked over to the bookshelves. To my delight, the shelves were filled with the classics; Pride and Prejudice, To Kill a Mockingbird, Gone with the Wind, among numerous others.

In the far corner tucked away was a small framed black and white photo of a beautiful young girl with flowing curls. I wondered if this could be Stella and almost dropped it when Ms. Carine asked me what I was holding.

I stammered and said, "I was looking at your vast collection of books when I saw this photo. Is this a picture of Stella?"

Ms. Carine gently took it from me and said, "Yes, this is Stella. She was 16 years old in this photo."

"Why, she's simply gorgeous!" I exclaimed. Much more beautiful than I ever imagined."

"Yes, she was beautiful. She was also wild and crazy. A dangerous combination for any woman," said Ms. Carine, with a smile on her face.

"Danielle, do you know what a woman's best attribute should be?" asked Ms. Carine.

"I would say a true and loving heart."

"Ms. Carine continued, "I believe a woman's best attribute is her brain, always her brain. Beauty can move mountains for a woman, but can only move them so far and for so long. Don't forget that beauty is fleeting, it is here and then it is gone. A true and loving heart is wonderful for the man she loves and gives her heart too. But don't forget. It doesn't mean that he will have that kind of heart for her. A woman that uses her brain will always come out on top. She can have everything and more. The first thing she has to do is figure out what she wants. If she can figure that out, the sky is the limit."

"You have it all figured out, don't you, Ms. Carine."

"Well when you live as long as I have, you begin to figure it out," she said as she laughed. When you have watched someone you love throw their life away, it makes you stop and think. Stella was born with it all: beauty, money, family, and brains. Something had to have happened to her when she was a little girl. I'm not sure what that could have been. She never shared it with me, but she deliberately put herself in danger time and time again. She was so cold inside, and that only comes from being hurt by someone you love. She threw her life away. It wasn't because she wasn't smart, but because she let her emotions rule the decisions she made, both good and bad.

I guess what I'm trying to say is that it's wonderful to be born with a good and loving heart, and if you're born a beauty, you are fortunate indeed. To be born into a family that has money has its advantages for sure. But a girl with brains can have all of it, if she uses her power wisely. It's important that she use her head to make important decisions, not her heart. Do you understand what I'm trying to tell you?"

"I think so, I said. That a woman should use her head to try and figure out a situation instead of relying on what her heart is telling her?"

Ms. Carine looked pleased and said, "Yes, Danielle, that's what I was trying to say. A heart that has been badly broken is never the same. It's like putting a puzzle together with a piece missing. You should love with your whole heart, but you should be smart enough to protect it from harm."

"Do you have any other pictures of Stella that I could see?" I asked.

"Yes, I do," said Ms. Carine, "Give me a minute, and I'll get them for you."

Ms. Carine walked out of the library and went into the kitchen. While she was gone, I had a chance to explore the library some more. In the corner of the room there was a lovely antique oak secretary desk with a drop leaf and a curio next to it. Sitting on top of the curio was an old lamp. Inside the desk was an inkwell and old stationary with the letter D embossed at the top of the paper. Inside the curio cabinet were tiny figurines of dogs and cats. I so wanted to open it and hold the figurines in my hand, but I didn't dare. There was a small black and white picture of a little girl sitting on a homemade bench. It was a tin lithograph, the first one I had ever seen. I wondered if this was a picture of Isabella. It was placed in the curio cabinet so I couldn't take it out to get a closer look.

Ms. Carine stepped up behind me and said, "What are you looking at, Danielle?"

I jumped at the sound of her voice and said, "I was just admiring your figurines and wondering who the little girl in the old tintype photograph was."

"That is my little girl Isabella at three years old," replied Ms. Carine, with so much sadness on her face. "Those figurines were gifts from her to me for my birthdays. She loved animals, and they loved her."

With that she walked away from me, and I knew that she didn't want to talk about Isabella yet.

She looked at me and said, "Here are a couple of pictures of Stella for you to look at."

She handed the first picture to me. It was Stella sitting on a horse in a riding outfit and boots. She had a cute riding hat, and her luxurious curls were spread over her shoulders. She had a small, tight smile on her face, but her eyes were ice cold. The second picture was a professional shot done in a studio. She had on a gorgeous, indigo blue dress that matched the color of her eyes. Her hair was piled high on her head, and there were hair pins with pearls placed in some of her curls. She wasn't smiling in this photo, and I found myself looking into her eyes trying to understand what she was thinking and what she was feeling.

"Is she everything you thought she would be?" asked Ms. Carine.

"Yes, and more," I replied, She is beautiful in an icy, cold way. Her smile never reaches her eyes."

"That is an accurate description of Stella," said Ms. Carine. Happiness eluded her all her life, as it does for most people who are born selfish. Selfish people can never be truly happy because they are never satisfied."

"And people who die young are always remembered that way. They never age," said Danielle.

"That is very true," said Ms. Carine. They remain young and beautiful forever in the memories of those that loved them. When every person that loved and grieved for them is gone, so is the memory of that person."

"That's right, especially when they don't have children and grandchildren to carry their bloodline and heritage into the ages," I said.

"Not everyone is fortunate enough to have a large family to carry on the family name. So many people have one or two children. If one perishes and the other doesn't marry, that is the end of that particular family. In the end, we are all forgotten. That is, unless you do something to make it into the history books."

"That is so depressing to think about, I said, to know that your life will be totally forgotten, as if you were never here at all. I'm beginning to understand why you feel the need to have your story told."

"Don't mind me, Danielle. When a person gets old he starts looking back on things. That's the reason why many people write their memoirs. They want the generations to come to have a chance to understand how life was before they were born. If they are fortunate their ancestors will also share the secrets kept hidden within their family."

"Danielle, are you ready to get back to my story?" asked Ms. Carine.

"Yes ma'am," I replied. She began speaking in a hushed voice.

This would be the last time that I would venture into the swamp alone. I felt as if I had trespassed onto private property, Edie's property.

I pushed Stella to the back of my mind and concentrated on my sweet daughter Isabella. I wanted time to slow down and keep her young forever. But as every mother knows, babies grow quickly, and my baby was no different. My favorite time of the day was early morning before anyone else was awake. I would sit in my bedroom looking out of the window while rocking my precious bundle of joy. I loved her so much that it was hard to remember life without her.

I thought about my mother and when she gave birth to me. How could she not love me and not want me? I would never understand it.

I wrote to let her know that she was a grandmother and gave her the news about Stella. I offered again to send someone there to pick her up and bring her here so that I could take care of her. I would not hold my breath on a response from her.

Joshua was once again distant, and several nights a week was nowhere to be found. I found myself jittery and anxious on the nights that he was away. What secret was he keeping from me?

CHAPTER ELEVEN

Mrs. Vernice had taken it upon herself to keep me occupied while he was out. We had started a puzzle of the moon and the stars. We worked on it in the evenings and even though we had nothing to say to one other, not being alone was soothing for both of us.

Isabella was a ruby in our family of pearls. Her infectious smile lit up the face of anyone who was near her. Her beauty and perfection captured the attention of anyone who gazed upon her. Mrs. Vernice adored her and held her in her arms every chance she got. We joked that this child would never learn to walk because we never put her down.

She was a good baby and was content in our arms or lying in her crib. Joshua had started spending time with her every day after he had his lunch. He walked the grounds with her and showed her off to all of the servants.

A date had been set, and plans had been made for Isabella's baptism. Isabella was now eight weeks old. It would be the first time that we received company since Stella's death. All of their cousins, aunts, and uncles had been invited, along with neighbors and friends. Mrs. Vernice had been busy sewing Isabella's christening gown which was adorned with delicate white embroidery, lace, and small pearls. I was crocheting her booties and cap from the finest of yarn and had sewed little pearls around the headband of the cap. Her christening gown, cap, and booties would be treasured and tucked safely away for the next baby, if ever there was another.

This was the day her soul would be pledged to the Lord in the sacrament of baptism, which was considered one of the most important days of her young life.

Her soul which was tainted by the original sin that we are all born with would be cleansed, thereby giving her the gift of salvation. We had the task of picking godparents for Isabella. I had written to my friend Bunetta and had asked her if she would agree to be my child's godmother or nanny as it was called here. Bunetta was swift in her reply and made plans to be here for that special day. She would visit with me for two weeks, and I was excited beyond belief.

Joshua asked his first cousin Andre to be the godfather. He stated that Andre was a good man and attended church faithfully. Robert had been sent to live with Mrs. Vernice's brother to help him with his farm. Joshua felt bad not asking his only brother but felt it would be in Isabella's best interest to have Andre as her godfather, or Paran, as was the custom title in the south. He and Bunetta would deny the devil and accept the Holy Spirit at her baptism on behalf of their little goddaughter.

Bunetta arrived at our home a couple of days before the baptism. She came alone as her husband was too busy with his practice to accompany her. She brought along her personal maid Ester. Ester and Rosa were the same age and inseparable during the time they were here.

Bunetta and I were ecstatic to see one another and jumped around like school girls. We went up to my bedroom, each of us sitting cross-legged on the bed and talking over one another. We both had so much to share. We talked for hours trying to catch up on our lives. Bunetta was dying to find out what had happened to Stella. Her eyes were as round as saucers as I shared the story with her. Joshua's demeanor was courteous but cool when he spoke to Bunetta. I was embarrassed by his actions, but Bunetta wasn't fazed.

Bunetta said, "Honey, when a man is threatened by his wife's female friend, it could mean one or two things. It may just be that he is insecure. Or he could be hiding something from you and he is afraid I will figure it out and enlighten you!"

"I laughed along with her but what she said interested me in many ways. I knew my husband was hiding something or someone from me, I just didn't know who or what it was.

"The next few weeks were busy ones at the plantation. Every inch of the house was scrubbed by the servants in preparation of the celebration. Meals were planned in advance, and home-made pralines were cooked and put aside for that special day.

The day before the celebration, the cooks, under the watchful eye of Mrs. Vernice, prepared and cooked the pies. Blackberry, fig, blueberry, and sweet potato pies filled the house with such a scrumptious scent it made your mouth water with the anticipation of eating them.

My father-in-law had been fattening a hog a few weeks before the celebration. The field hands were up at dawn to kill and get the hog ready for the boucherie. Not one piece of the hog was wasted in the pig roast. They made boudin and cracklings early that morning. Bunetta said that she had never tasted anything as good as this. As little as she was, I was always amazed at how much food this girl could consume.

We rode to the old Catholic Church that was built along the bayou. The church was filled with our family and friends. Some came by carriage, and some traveled by pirogue. The sunlight resonated through the stained glass windows casting prisms on the floor. It was a special day and everyone was dressed in their Sunday best.

Bunetta held Isabella while the priest poured holy water over my newborn baby's head. Isabella had just received her first sacrament. The original sin she was born with had been washed away from her soul through the sacrament of baptism. It was a very special day and

I felt relieved knowing that my baby's soul had been washed clean, God forbid, should anything ever happen to her.

We returned to the plantation, and the celebration began. The band set up their instruments under the old oak tree in the back yard. The fiddle was played by Joshua's Uncle Stan or Noc Stan, as he was called. His Aunt Dell or as he called her Tant Dell played the accordion. His cousin George sang all the French songs that they loved so much. Everyone grabbed a partner and danced the two-step in the yard, kicking up dust and getting drunk on homemade wine.

"Did you understand French at all, Ms. Carine?" asked Danielle.

Ms. Carine threw her head back and laughed. "The first few years not at all," she said. "I didn't talk much back then but I sure as hell listened. It used to irritate me so. I thought them so rude to speak French in front of me. They knew I didn't know what they were talking about.

"Then one day, I realized that I did understand what they were saying. Cajuns speak a broken language, half-English and half-French. After listening to their conversations for a couple of years, everything they were saying had sunk in. I now understood what they were saying in French but wasn't about to let them know it."

"Did you ever learn to speak it?" I asked.

"No, said Ms. Carine. I never tried. I was content just knowing what was being said. Besides, when they spoke to me, they always addressed me in English."

"Did Bunetta understand French?"

"No, not at all, laughed Ms. Carine, But how she loved to hear them speak. She thought of those Cajuns as completely foreign. She made me tell her everything they were saying, especially if they were talking about her!"

Mrs.Vernice tried her best not to like her but Bunetta would not leave the poor woman alone. She was determined to get Mrs. Vernice to talk to her and followed her around the house asking her a million questions. She was very interested in how Mrs. Vernice ran the household. Bunetta confessed to me that she was a terrible head mistress and that her husband had taken on that task too. She vowed that when she left Louisiana she would leave trained by Mrs.Vernice to go home and run a tight ship. Mrs.Vernice fussed about it but I think she was secretly pleased to pass on her managing skills especially since neither Stella nor I had ever been interested in learning.

Bunetta thought that Isabella was the most beautiful baby she had ever laid eyes on. She spent very little time holding or rocking her though. Bunetta was much more interested in riding and exploring the plantation and meeting people.

Always aware of other people's feelings she sensed mine and said, "Carine I have three little boys at home. Those boys are always needing something and they wear me out. When I do get time away from them, I selfishly think only of myself and my needs.

"You and I will make plans to visit each other several times a year. Our children will grow up knowing one another, we will make sure of that. But right now Isabella is too little to even know that I am here, true? So you and I will visit and spend our precious time together and have some fun, okay?"

Bunetta could always calm any fears that I had. She could also talk me into doing things I normally wouldn't. I guess you could say she was a bad influence, at least that's what Joshua used to say. I loved her energy and her spirit. Every day was an adventure with my new-found friend. She made friends easily which was not the case for me. I met more people when Bunetta was visiting than I had in all the years I lived here.

Bunetta laughed and said, "There's no secret to getting people to talk Carine. Just ask whoever you are talking too about themselves, people love to talk about themselves! You don't have to listen to what they say. Believe me they won't even notice that you're not listening to them, they will just keep on talking.

After we would spend time talking to all these people we would then slip away by ourselves and laugh and make fun of them. I knew it was juvenile and silly but Bunetta made it fun. It was a secret that the two of us shared.

When she got ready to go home, I begged her to stay for another week. But she couldn't stay. She had three children and a husband to see about. We made plans for Isabella and I to visit her six months from now in Mississippi. She invited Joshua to come along and he said he would think about it.

I cried when Bunetta left. It would be unbearably lonely without her here. However, knowing that I would see her again gave me something to look forward to. After having Bunetta here the last two weeks, it would be very quiet without her. She taught me that if you want to have friends, sometimes you have to make the first move. She made me promise her that I would go and visit several of the women I had met at the baptism. I told her I would try.

Before Bunetta left, she took me aside and said, "Your husband is indeed hiding something from you. He is a very private man and doesn't share his thoughts easily. Try to talk him in to coming with you when you visit me. My Henry is a likeable fellow and will have Joshua eating out of his hand. I promise you that before you leave my home, we will have uncovered his secret, or at least we will have a better idea of what he is hiding."

"I had to ask myself if I really wanted to know what my husband was hiding from me. What would I do then? When things hidden came to light, would I then be forced to make a decision? I would have to live with the knowledge of what my husband was doing or I would have to leave him, the father of my baby? I had to slow my thoughts down.

"I was getting ahead of myself. I needed to look at the facts, as I knew them. What I did know was that Joshua spent most nights somewhere else. I felt that he was in love but not with me. He treated me like I was an acquaintance, just someone he knew. His heart belonged to someone, but whom?

"I would drive myself crazy thinking about this so I put it out of my mind for now. I had a baby girl to see about, and her welfare was my concern. I can do this, I thought. I've been doing it for all these years. And I did.

"I concentrated on Isabella and my plans to visit Bunetta, and the days flew by. I made a point of visiting a couple of Joshua's cousins. After all, they had invited me to stop by.

"Joshua's cousin Claire lived in a three storied home in the middle of the woods in Bayou Chicot. She had never married and had inherited her family's home. I have to admit I almost turned around when I got there.

"She was a bit of an eccentric and lived all alone in that big spooky house. She read tarot cards and told fortunes. That was how she made extra money. She offered to read my cards, but I turned her down," said Ms. Carine.

"Why didn't you want your cards read?" I asked.

"I was afraid," said Ms. Carine.

"What were you afraid of?"

"I'm not sure. I think I was afraid of what she would see in my past. My father was a gypsy and my mother, an adulterer. Not a past I was proud of. And certainly not a past that I wanted Joshua's family to gossip about behind my back," said Ms. Carine.

At that instant, I felt a hand touch my shoulder, and I jumped out of my chair. It was Rosa and I swear she did it on purpose.

She said "Why, Ms. Danielle, you sure are jumpy. Are you okay?"

I responded with, "Yes, I'm alright. You just startled me, is all."

"I just wanted to remind you of the time. It's getting dark outside. I know you hate to leave here after dark," said Rosa.

"Thank you for thinking of me, Rosa." I replied, a little sarcastically. I looked at Ms. Carine with a sweet smile and said, I will see you next week."

Ms. Carine smiled and said, "Come early next week, Rosa will make a special breakfast for us."

Rosa, with a scowl on her face, said, "That's right, I will make a wonderful breakfast for you."

As I was leaving, I turned around and asked Ms. Carine a question. "Ms. Carine, I've noticed that you had beautiful paintings hanging in your house. I was wondering who painted them?"

She said, "I painted all of them years ago."

"I didn't know that you were an artist," I replied, I'm so impressed!"

She smiled and said, "Thank you. I haven't painted in years because of my arthritis and all. But thank you for noticing."

I picked up my purse and coat and left to go home. The sun was setting, and I walked around the house to watch it. In an instant I was transported to the past, and the fields were backlit with the setting sun. As far as my eyes could see were acres of fluffy, white cotton plants in bloom. Field hands were walking out of the cotton fields carrying tools and bags. Some were talking and laughing, and a few were singing hymns.

Then this vision was gone, and I was standing alone in the dark. I felt like crying, and I wanted to go back. I looked toward the house, and Rosa was watching me through the window, smiling and shaking her head. I jumped in my car and headed home. I was in awe of what had just happened to me. For a brief moment, I was at the plantation in its glory days. Why was this happening to me? It was as if something or someone was trying to pull me back in time. I shook my head to clear it and got in my car and headed home.

On Monday I was quiet at work, and of course Justine noticed.

As soon as we had a break, she looked at me and said, "Spill it."

I said, "I don't know what you mean."

"Why are you so quiet today?" asked Justine. Did something bad happen that I'm not aware of?"

"No, nothing bad happened, I said. I just had a different kind of experience, is all."

"Okay, am I going to have to drag this out of you?" asked Justine.

"No, but I'm worried that you will think that I'm slowly losing my mind. The other evening when I was leaving Ms. Carine's, I stopped to admire the sunset behind her house. All of a sudden, I had a vision of standing in that exact spot a hundred years ago.

The cotton fields were snowy white with cotton blooms as far as my eyes could see. I could hear voices, and then I saw field hands emerging from the fields with their cotton sacks and tools. Coming out of the fields, were a couple of women, holding hands singing a gospel hymn. It was all so real and I felt like I was home again.

I looked at Justine out of the corner of my eyes to try and gage her reaction. I have to give it to her, she was trying her best not to over react.

"So are you making plans to put me away anytime soon?" I asked.

"No, said Justine, "but, wow, this is a lot to take in. You need to give me a few minutes to think about what you just said."

So we sat in silence for a few minutes. I was already regretting telling her. Then she turned and looked at me.

"Look," said Justine, "we need to put all of this into perspective. First you meet this old lady at the doctor's office. You help her, and she invites you to her house for a thank-you visit. From that moment on, you are at her house every single weekend. The first time you visit her, you see a child that no one else sees. You see a ghost that committed suicide in that same house. Then you see her a second time! Now you say that you had a vision of cotton fields and slaves, and to top it all off, you feel like you belonged there!" exclaimed Justine. Should I be worried, you tell me."

CHAPTER TWELVE

"MY BIRTHDAY"

"I admit it sounds insane, I said, But, I can't help but believe it is all happening for a reason. I just haven't figured it out yet."

"After that day, I found myself pulling away from Justine. Sharing these things with her was making me feel uncomfortable, as though something was wrong with me.

"Instinctively, I started to build a wall around myself. I decided not to share what was going on with Justine or anyone else. From now on, I would write whatever I needed to share, and I would figure this out on my own. Paranoia had begun to set in and following it was confusion with anger close by. I feared I was losing my mind, but my involvement was too deep to stop now.

Saturday morning finally got here, and I was up before daylight. I took a quick shower hoping it would help me wake up. I wanted to get to Ms. Carine's house before they were up so that I could snoop around outside. I got to Ms. Carine's house before the light of day. The private drive to her house seemed different today, unkempt and abandoned.

When I got closer to her house, I panicked. In the near distance, the house looked like a shell of its former self. The porch had rotted away and was falling in on itself. Most of the steps on the stairway outside going into the attic were missing. The beautiful, big windows were broken, and glass was strewn everywhere. Trees and vines had taken over the exterior of the majestic old place.

I blinked, and everything was back to normal. I could see smoke rising out of the chimney, and the light in the windows was a welcoming sight. At that moment, I feared for my sanity. When I was last here, I went back to a time when the plantation was bustling with activity. Somehow, today I saw into the future. I envisioned a time into the future when the house was neglected and abandoned.

Before I could question what I had just seen, I noticed something white moving in the distance. I parked my car and peered into the window to see if Rosa had seen me drive up. She was nowhere around. I quietly walked to the back yard, looking through the mist searching for the little girl. I had a feeling that what I had spotted was her white dress.

I quietly walked to the backyard, staying close to the house so as not to be seen. I spotted the little girl a few feet away. She didn't notice me. She was playing with the black child I had seen her with a few months ago. They were tossing stones into the pond. Both were oblivious to my presence. They broke out in a game of chase and ran, playing in the field.

I turned toward the old wrought iron fence and started to walk there. At that moment, I heard Rosa calling out to me.

"Ms. Danielle, you sure are early today. I guess you are anxious to eat some of that special breakfast Ms. Carine had me cook for y'all. "

I turned around, looking guilty because I had gotten caught. Rosa was at the back door holding it open for me to enter. She didn't scold me for being where I shouldn't have been. She knew that she had caught me red-handed, and apparently today that was enough.

I didn't bother telling her that I had seen the two little girls playing in the back yard. It didn't matter anyway because she couldn't see them, and she didn't believe me.

Ms. Carine was sitting at the breakfast table drinking a cup of coffee and waiting on me. Rosa had outdone herself this morning. She had prepared a feast of creamy corn grits, bacon, eggs, and pancakes. We sat in silence and ate.

Rosa said, "It must be good cause y'all ain't talking, y'all just eating."

I replied, "Yes ma'am, it is delicious. Thank you for cooking all of this food. I don't believe I've told you that today is my birthday"

Ms. Carine smiled and said, "Danielle you are a sweet and appreciative girl. Your friendship means so much to me. I want to wish a happy birthday to my special friend. May we never take for granted the friendships that we form."

"Thank you, Ms. Carine. Your friendship is also very special to me," I replied.

"If you don't mind me asking, said Ms. Carine, How is your book coming along?"

Surprised at her question, I replied. "I'm writing down everything that you are telling me. If I possess the talent to turn your story into a book is yet to be seen."

"I have complete confidence in your abilities," said Ms. Carine. Danielle, you need to learn to trust yourself."

"I'm working on that, Ms. Carine, but it doesn't happen overnight."

"Confidence in oneself is built day by day, and by your experiences. I want you to trust yourself the way that I trust you. And, because you are here so early, we'll have a full day, said Ms. Carine. Let's go into the library and make ourselves comfortable so we can begin."

I excused myself and went to the bathroom. This time I kept eyes opened. I didn't want any surprises. As I washed my hands in the sink, I looked in the mirror and kept my eyes on the bathtub. For just an instant, in the corner of the mirror, I thought I saw a red curl. Looking at the mirror again, it was gone.

Rosa was standing outside of the door when I came out. She raised her eyebrows in a questioning look. I just ignored her and kept walking to the library. I went in and sat in the old rocker. There was a fresh cup of coffee waiting for me. Ms. Carine smiled at me and began her story.

"I know that everyone believes that their baby is perfect and the most beautiful baby in the world. But, in my case, it was true, she said with a twinkle in her eye. Let me tell you a little about Isabella.

"She kept a serious look on her sweet little face and seemed to be interested in what was being said to her. This, in turn, caused many an adult to talk to her about what was on their minds.

"She heard about illnesses and how the crops were doing. She heard people's problems and shared in their joy. When someone needed comforting she seemed to know and always wrapped her fat little arms around their necks with a tight hug. When they needed cheering up, she was silly and made them laugh. Her little dimples always invoked a smile. She had a calming effect on anyone who was around her. It was her gift. She loved sitting on everyone's lap while she played quietly with her toys. My baby girl had something I never had, and that was love, pure and simple.

"When Isabella was eight months old, we took our trip to Mississippi to visit Bunetta. Joshua opted out, saying he was too busy at work. He promised to come and visit our last week there. I had arranged to stay with Bunetta and her family for one month.

"Bunetta had gone out of her way to make me feel welcome. A dinner party had been planned for my first week there. She was looking forward to introducing me to her family and friends. She was excited to show off her only godchild.

"Bunetta and Henry lived in the city in a gorgeous three-story brick home. There was an inner courtyard filled with stately magnolia trees and exquisite roses of every color. At the far end of the courtyard, jasmine vines climbed the old brick walls.

"In the center of it, there was an enormous water fountain with a statue of a mother and her two children. She was holding a watering can that was pouring water back into the fountain.

"Henry's office was located at the back of the house, with an entrance there. Two benches had been placed outside of the door.

Bunetta said his patients arrived before he opened his door, and the benches were for their comfort.

"An old gardenia bush was planted in the back, giving off a sweet fragrance. Baskets of ferns hung everywhere. It was a well-thought out and lovely entrance to a doctor's office. I will admit that I was impressed.

"Rosa, of course, had accompanied me on the trip, I never traveled without her. We shared a room on the second floor. A trundle bed was brought in for her so that she could care for Isabella. All of the house servants slept on the third floor.

"Bunetta's home was located in the middle of town. Every afternoon we strolled down the city sidewalks and visited with her neighbors. There was a park across the street from their home. Rosa brought Isabella to the park everyday along with Bunetta's children and their nanny.

"Dress shops were located only a couple of blocks away. Bunetta and I frequented a different store every day. At first I was aghast at the amount of money that she spent. It's amazing how quickly a person can get accustomed to a certain lifestyle. I found myself envious of my friend and of her life in a big city.

"Henry was a likable fellow, although I found him a bit scatterbrained. He spoiled Bunetta tremendously, and his favorite quote was "Anything for my girl".

Their boys were adorable, and they fell in love with Isabella, or Izzy, as they had fondly started calling her. It was a nickname that would stay with her the rest of her life.

Bunetta's dinner party was a success, or so she thought. Her closest friend Renella was very interested in meeting me, but for all the wrong reasons. I got the third degree from her and then she snubbed her nose at me. She was Bunetta's oldest and closest friend, and she let me know that would never change. She didn't appreciate me butting in on their friendship. She also insinuated that I had my eye on Bunetta's husband.

I let her know that I had a husband of my own, and was not interested in any other man, thank you. I was offended by her and what she was falsely accusing me of. I tried not to let her get to me. After all, I was here for only a short while.

"A few days after the party, Renella tried to make plans for the three of us to spend the day together. I made several excuses why I couldn't attend. Bunetta was suspicious and started asking questions. I finally admitted what had happened at the dinner party. She was angry and left to confront her old friend.

"When she returned, she said that everything had been worked out with Renella. She said that she was a very insecure person and had gotten jealous of me. Bunetta had assured her that she had room in her heart for many friends. I was relieved. I didn't want to be the cause of any problems between them. Bunetta also laughed at Renella's accusation regarding Henry. She believed that she had Henry firmly wrapped around her little finger. He would never dare look at another woman. The idea was ridiculous to her. She made sure that Renella understood that.

"The shopping trip was planned for Friday. I went with the best intentions to try and get along with this woman. We dined at a fancy restaurant, and I thought, this will be good. As long as Bunetta was with us, Renella acted decently toward me. When Bunetta went to the restroom, things changed drastically.

Renella leaned in close to me and whispered, "I know what you're trying to do, but I won't let you!"

I said, "I have no idea what you are trying to accuse me of now."

"You are trying to get in between my friendship with Bunetta," whispered Renella. I see through your plans and believe me, I will stop you cold!"

"Before I could answer her, Bunetta was back and Renella started laughing and joking as if she had never said a word to me. I was uneasy the rest of the day and made an excuse to leave early. Bunetta insisted on leaving with me, and Renella gave me a bone chilling look of disgust.

On our walk home, Bunetta insisted that I tell her what had happened between Renella and me while she was in the bathroom. I swore to her that nothing had happened, but she wouldn't buy it.

She said, "I know Renella, and I know how her mind works. I can handle that girl and her mouth. I just need to know what filth came out of it while I was away from the table."

I then repeated what Renella had said.

She smiled and said, "Please don't trouble your mind with this nonsense for a minute longer. I will handle Renella."

When we got back to Bunetta's house, we sat in the courtyard and had sweet tea while we played with our children. I realized at that moment that I had hardly seen my child while I was here. I felt a strong urge to return home back to my normal life.

Bunetta, always perceptive to my feelings, said, "Tomorrow we will take the children to the beach. We need to spend some quality time with these kiddos."

I sighed with relief and said, "I would love that more than anything."

We spent the next week at home with the children and I started feeling more comfortable.

After one week of spending time with the kids, I could see that Bunetta was getting restless. She wasn't used to staying home and dealing with children. Maybe she was tired of us being here and having to entertain me. All I know is that I started to see a different side to my friend. She spoke to me in an aggravated tone of voice. She said she was going out for a while and would be back later.

I spent the rest of the afternoon with my daughter, and we stayed in our bedroom for supper. Later that evening, Henry knocked lightly on my door.

"I'm sorry to disturb you Carine, but can you tell me where my wife is tonight?" asked Henry.

"I don't know where she is," I replied. "I think she needed time to herself. She has been entertaining me for the last few weeks," I said laughingly.

Henry looked at me with a knowing look on his face and sadness in his eyes. He said, "Yes, that must be it. She's not used to staying home every day. She is a woman that relishes her freedom. I'm sure she will be back soon."

Later that evening, much later, I heard both of them yelling. He was demanding to know where she had been and with whom. She said she had been with her best friend Renella at her home. She said Renella was threatened by her friendship with me and she needed to spend time with her to qualm her fears. If he didn't believe it, all he had to do was call her. He stormed out of their bedroom and slammed the door. At that moment, I wished that I was home.

The last week of our visit, Joshua showed up. My extreme happiness at his arrival surprised and delighted him. We had one more week here and then we could head back home.

Henry was a perfect host, and he and Joshua made fast friends. I could tell that Bunetta was sorry for the way she had acted and was trying to make it up to me.

I asked her what she and Renella had spoken about the other night.

She laughed and said, "Carine, you are such an innocent. I didn't go to Renella's house. I'm still angry with that girl. I will deal with her later."

"Where were you then, and why did you lie to your husband?"

"Do you really want to know where I was or with whom? Because I will tell you and you probably won't approve," replied Bunetta looking at me out the corner of her eye.

"Yes, I want to know, even if I won't like it," I said. Stella used to accuse me of sticking my head in the sand, and not living in the real world. I'm a big girl. Tell me where you were and what you were doing."

"You promise you won't hold it against me or think differently about me, asked Bunetta?"

I took a deep breath and said, "I promise."

"I was strolling down the river, having a stimulating conversation with another man," admitted Bunetta. Anything more than that is not your business."

"Why would you do that?" I exclaimed. Don't you love Henry?"

"Why, don't be silly, Carine. Of course, I love my Henry. It's just that I need more."

"He gives you everything you need. What else could you want?"

"I don't know," said Bunetta, I'm just never satisfied with what I have."

"You're a spoiled brat is what you are," I exclaimed. That man is so good to you, too good!"

"Now Carine, you promised not to judge and I believe that's what you're doing," said Bunetta.

"I just don't understand why you need more, when you have so much more than most women could dream of having," I said.

"Okay let's not talk about it again, said Bunetta. Stick your head in the sand. You're much happier there."

"I am, and I will," I said, and I stormed off to my room.

Joshua noticed how upset I was and asked what was upsetting me. I just told him I was tired, and I was ready to go home. He said that we would leave early Saturday morning.

I broke the news to Bunetta the next morning. She said she understood our need to get back home. We packed up the children and had a picnic at the lake. Henry closed the office, and we made a day of it. Bunetta spent more time playing with Izzy than she had the whole time we were here.

At the end of the day, she hugged me tightly and said, "Not all women are as pure of heart as you are, my dear friend. So, as my friend and the good Christian woman that you are, I would hope for your prayers and not your judgement."

"Are you sorry for what you've done to your husband behind his back?" I asked her.

"Only if I get caught!" laughed Bunetta.

"You are just ridiculous," I screamed. Then we both laughed. I didn't agree with what she was doing, and I knew that she would get caught eventually. Henry was already suspicious.

She said, "Are we still friends? I am your daughter's godmother, after all."

"I looked at her, smiled and said, "Yes, we're still friends. But lord help you if you do get caught and lose the wonderful life you've been blessed with. You can't say I didn't warn you."

"That's not for you to worry about, said Bunetta. I just want you to be my friend."

"We left Natchez the next day, and I breathed a sigh of relief. It occurred to me that Bunetta didn't mention if she had figured out my husband's secret. After hearing her secret, I wasn't sure if I could handle knowing what my husband was hiding.

"I was unusually quiet on the trip back home. Joshua noticed and asked if Bunetta and I had gotten into a disagreement. I told him that we had, but it was a trivial matter. I said that we had spent too much time together, and we needed to get back to our own lives. I could tell that he knew that there was more to this story, but for the moment he would leave it alone.

"I was happy to return to the plantation, which I had grown to love. I spent the next several months spending time with Izzy. She was growing so fast that it was hard to keep up with her. Joshua had started horseback riding with her every morning and afternoon to check on the cotton fields. I started helping Mrs. Vernice manage the household, and that made her extremely happy. She was not feeling well as of late. I noticed that she had started slowing down. While Robert living at her brother's house had helped her tremendously, she still missed him terribly. He was her child, and she was worried about him. Now that I had a child, I could understand how she felt.

"Before we knew it, Izzy's first birthday was here. Her birthday would always be clouded with pain because it was also the day that we lost Stella. Mrs. Vernice's mind seemed to be slipping more each day.

"I noticed that she couldn't remember the ingredients in the recipes that she had cooked all of her life. I tried to talk to Joshua about her problem, but he thought I was exaggerating the situation. I took charge of her birthday party and invited their family and friends.   .

"She had a wonderful day, and so did everyone else. As we were saying our goodbyes to the last of our guests, I realized that I hadn't seen Mrs. Vernice since earlier that day. I went through the house looking for her, but she wasn't there. I finally found her wandering along the bayou. I asked her what she was doing out here all alone. She looked at me and said, "I'm looking for that child. I can't keep track of her. Then she started calling, Stella! Stella! It's time to come home, child!"

"I took her by the arm and led her back home. I assured her that I would find Stella. I had Lydia put her to bed, and I sent for the doctor. He explained that sometimes when people get older their minds start to falter. He said that this was the anniversary of Stella's death, and that might be affecting her state of mind. He gave her a mild sedative and said he would check on her later this week.

"After that day, she was never the same. I took over the household and the managing of the servants. Most days, Mrs. Vernice sat in the rocker on the porch and played with Izzy. As the weeks and months passed, the fog in her mind got deeper. Every once in a while she would recognize Isabella, but most days she called her Stella. Joshua and his father didn't deal with this situation. That was left in my hands.

"I wondered how I had gotten myself into this situation again. I had spent my childhood taking care of my mother. Now, I found myself taking care of my mother in-law. Life had come full circle with me in the middle taking care of another woman who never cared for me.

"How did I get here? I wondered. This is not how my life was supposed to be. My days were so busy running the house that I didn't have any time to spend with my baby girl. Then it occurred to me that Mrs. Vernice was no longer in charge, I was. I could make my own rules. So I did.

"I put Lydia in charge of the household duties with the understanding that she would report to me daily. All decisions or changes would be made by me only. We hired a new maid named Millie to take Lydia's place and Lydia was in charge of her training. Lydia's status with the staff was raised, and everyone was happy.

"I was there at all times, but I was doing the things I loved to do.

I went back to my flower garden, and I began to experiment with paints. The results are what you see hanging on my walls.

Mrs. Vernice had begun to share things with me that was pressing on her mind, things I wished I'd never heard. She told me stories of how she locked Stella up in a dark closet when she was bad and that Mr. Sterling wasn't Stella's daddy, a salesman passing through was. I tried to make her stop but she just kept on talking and unburdening her conscience on me. She said that Robert molested so many young girls, maybe even Stella, she wasn't sure. Then she said that Stella was just born bad. Oh how that hurt me, how can a child be born bad? I was beginning to understand why Stella's heart was ice-cold. Mrs. Vernice said I would truly understand when I found her statement in the safe where she'd put it. There was no safe or none that I was aware of. She never would tell me where this safe was located. I asked Joshua and he said there was no such safe in this house. So I let it go.

"The years rolled by so quickly that I lost track of time. When I turned around, Isabella was six years old and the reigning beauty of the parish! We had buried Mrs. Vernice two years before and Mr. Sterling, a year later. Mrs. Vernice had forgotten how to breathe, and we found her one morning in her bed. From what the doctor said, she had passed during the night. A year later, Mr. Sterling died in his sleep. "Like a candle in the wind" is how our prestigious doctor described his death.

"After Joshua's parents died, he withdrew even more from our loveless marriage. The only thing that kept us together was our daughter. She was the one thing we had in common. She loved both of us unconditionally, and she was the joy in our life.

"It had gotten so that Joshua and I were arguing over the smallest of things. We just couldn't hold a conversation between us, it seemed. If he said white, I said black. If he said stop, I'd say go. You get the idea. We disagreed about everything that we discussed.

"I like to say that Isabella was born with an old soul, said Ms. Carine. Do you understand what I mean by that?" she asked.

"I'm not sure I do," I replied.

"Even though she was just a child she had a certain level of wisdom that was much older than her years. She communicated well with the people around her and she had an enormous amount of empathy for them. It's what drew everyone to her. She was wise for someone so young. I guess you could say that I was wound up tight but I didn't realize it at the time.

"How seldom we see ourselves as we really are. It's so much easier to look at others and judge them for their shortcomings, and never recognize the characteristics that we despise in ourselves.

"A marriage between two people is hard work with much compromising. When you have love between you anything can be worked out. When there is no love it is almost impossible to conquer the hurdles in a marriage. Once a child is involved the dynamics change, and you are now a family. The needs of that child come first. If you are unhappy you push those feelings aside and you concentrate on your child. What you don't realize is how this unhappiness between you and your husband affects your child, and puts them in the middle.

"Our lives pass by quickly without us noticing it happening. My responsibilities were overseeing the servants, and making sure that they were doing their jobs. I had a daughter to raise and educate. I wanted to make sure that she would be well rounded in her education and the arts. Joshua ran the plantation and disappeared most evenings like he always had.

I no longer cared about where he spent his evenings and with whom. All I knew was when he was here, I felt as if I were walking on eggshells. The tension between us was so great. I didn't have to open my mouth to make him angry. A look was all it took.

"It affected Isabella greatly. Many nights after I tucked her in for the night I could hear her speaking softly. The first time it happened I quietly walked up to her door so that I could listen. She was on her knees next to her bed saying her prayers, asking God to help Mommy and Daddy love one another again. The poor child never knew that her Daddy didn't love me. His heart if he had one at all, I sometimes wondered, was promised to someone else. Why he had not married this other person was a great mystery to me.

"At the beginning I loved Joshua or so I thought I did. Now that I am old, it has occurred to me that I have never known what a man's love feels like.

"I would not change my past if I could, because to do so would be to not have had Isabella. I have many regrets, but she is certainly not one of them.

CHAPTER THIRTEEN

"ISABELLA"

"Why did you stay with him?" I asked.

"In those days, Danielle, people stuck it out. They stayed together on the good days and the bad days. We didn't have any family but each other. My mother had passed away years ago, and so had his. I guess we were what you would call nowadays a dysfunctional family," she said as she laughed.

"Rosa walked into the room at that point and said that lunch was ready. We went into the kitchen and ate. I wondered if Rosa and Ms. Carine ate their meals together when I wasn't there. Rosa had never sat and ate anything with us. I could feel Rosa's eyes on me so I turned to look at her. What I saw made my skin crawl with fear. I could see through her. She was translucent. The only thing solid on her were her eyes, and they were burning bright. I blinked, and she was normal again.

"I felt like I was walking on shaky ground, like things were shifting under me.

Ms. Carine said, "Are you feeling alright dear?"

I mumbled, "Yes, I just feel a little dizzy, that's all."

Ms. Carine said, "Rosa, grab a cold wet cloth to put on her head will you?" Rosa made her way to the sink and wet a washcloth which she brought to me.

I washed my face with the wet cloth and then announced that I felt much better. The truth was that I was feeling strange, and my legs were weak. I walked to the window and laid my head against the glass. When I opened my eyes, the little girl was standing in the backyard pointing to the graveyard with a look of urgency on her face. I looked at Ms. Carine and Rosa.

"They were both looking outside, but neither of them could see her. I felt like I was all alone in that kitchen and it disturbed me.

Ms. Carine said, "Danielle, do you feel like hearing more or do you need to go home to rest?"

"Oh no, I said, I'm fine, although it was a lie, because I was anything but fine.

"My head was spinning, and I felt like I was drugged. But I knew without a doubt that time was short, and Ms. Carine needed to finish her story. We went into the formal living room this time, and I felt somewhat better. This room wasn't as dark and dreary as the library.

Ms. Carine went on with her story right where she had left off.

"When Joshua and I would start bickering with one another, Isabella would step in and ask her father to take her for a ride on his horse. She knew that he would never refuse her. Sometimes, she would take my hand and say, "Mother, let's go and cut some fresh flowers for our dinner table." We unknowingly had placed our child in the middle of our discontent.

One morning she asked to go and play with one of the children on the farm. I suggested to Joshua that he go and get the little girl and bring her here so I could keep an eye on them. I didn't let her roam the farm like Stella had done. Joshua had to go to town to pick up supplies, and the two girls begged to ride with him.

It was summer, and it was stifling hot that year. It drained every ounce of energy in my body. Joshua took the girls with him, and said he'd be back in an hour or so. I finished up in my flower beds, then took a bath, and laid down for a nap. A nap nowadays was a luxury and not something I took often. I informed Lydia that the girls were with Joshua in town, and I was lying down for a nap. She was to wake me when they got back.

"I woke up to a child screaming. Confused and not sure of where the screaming was coming from, I ran down the stairs and through the house slamming the backdoor. In the distance, I could see Cammie standing in the pond staring at the water screaming. My heart was thumping so hard in my chest that her screams sounded far away. When I got to the edge of the pond, I saw Isabella floating face down in that dirty water. I jumped in the water to save her. I had never learned to swim but in my mind, I could and would swim to her. I finally reached my precious child and grabbed her and somehow pulled her out of that dark nasty water.

"Where was everyone? Where was Joshua, I couldn't understand. I screamed for him while I held my precious daughter but he never came. I pleaded with God to give my daughter back as I held her small cold body close to mine.

"When the realization of what just happened became clear, I tried bargaining with God. My life: for hers. I ran back into the pond intending to drown myself, but they pulled me out. The only thing I was sure of was that I couldn't live without her in my life. The sky began to blacken around me and then darkness crept into my soul.

"I felt disconnected from this world and as my mind began to break, for me, time stood still.

"I listened as the sounds of anguished screams slowly dissipated leaving only a muffled sound in its place. It was as if there were two soft hands being held over my ears. The feeling was soothing and I welcomed it. My breath was shallow and quiet, my heart so badly broken that I felt it was torn in two.

"I willed myself to die, it was a death, I would have accepted. To my dismay, my heart kept beating and I kept breathing. As grief consumed me, I slowly sank into the depths of shock. It was much too horrible for my mind to understand. Accidents always are.

"How could I understand my little girl of six was here with me one minute and then gone in the next? I had no one to turn too, no one that I could share my pain with. My journey to hell had begun.

"I couldn't remember anything after I found her. I convinced myself that I had saved her and she was alive. I was told that by the time Joshua arrived from the barn, he found Isabella dead in one of the servant's arms and Lydia trying to save my life. They all knew that she was gone.

"When I dove into the water the first time, Cammie ran to the servants to get help, but it was already too late. When I dove in the second time to drown myself, they were there to save me. Unbeknownst to any of us, Joshua had dropped the girls off earlier at the front door while he had driven to the barn to unload the supplies. They had been told to go inside of the house and let me know that they were home. Instead they let me sleep and went out to the pond to play.

"After her death I remained in a catatonic state and the doctor's prognosis was that I suffered a nervous breakdown. He convinced Joshua that I was in need of twenty-four hour care and that I needed to be admitted to a sanitarium.

"It didn't take much coaxing for Joshua to put me away in a mental asylum. He blamed me for napping that day and I blamed him for dropping them off. It was a load off of his shoulders to have me gone, and so, I remained there for the next twenty years. The doctors at the asylum gave me a doll. For a short while it seemed to soothe me and I kept it next to me, night and day. At first I was happy with what I thought was my little girl at my side. But the gnawing sadness in my soul overwhelmed me and would not leave so easily.

"At certain moments, I would regain clarity from the drugs being administered to me, and the events of that day would come rushing back, knocking me to my knees with grief. How can any mother accept the death of her child. Her love was the only love I had ever known.

"I thought of my mother and the children she had buried and I was ashamed of my indifference to her pain.

"The nurses there were quick to administer the medicine to numb my senses and keep me quiet. Keeping quiet was very important in this place. I didn't mind it so much. I willingly succumbed to the darkness with relief.

"As the years slowly moved on I began to accept what had happened to Isabella but there was bitterness in my soul. I couldn't comprehend that a loving God would take my child away. The faith that I had spent my entire life building began to crumble. I blamed God for the accident and her death. If he truly loved me, he would have spared her life. I worked myself up into such fits that they kept me sedated and at times in a straight-jacket, so that I would not harm myself.

"As soon as the fog created by the drugs would begin to lift, my mind would begin spinning out of control. Somewhere along that time, I decided that I had been wrong all along. It wasn't God's fault that Isabella had died. How could it be his fault when he didn't exist? It was then that I found regret and bitterness had seeped into my very being, and I descended further into the depths of despair.

"After many years, the doctors there began to see improvements in my behavior, and they felt that I was finally on my way to recovery. I recognized that the little girl sitting on my lap was not Isabella and only a doll. The doctor saw that recognition as a positive thing. He pursued an aggressive form of therapy with me and started by telling me what had really happened when I found Isabella in the pond.

"The doctor informed me that I dove into the water to save Isabella, only to start drowning myself. I grabbed Isabella by her dress and when Lydia pulled me out, she pulled Isabella out too. When Joshua got to the pond he watched as Lydia worked on saving me. He did nothing but watch.

It was too late for Isabella. She had been under the water for too long by the time I got to her.

"After a few weeks they knew I wasn't going to come out of it, and Joshua made his decision to put me away.

"It's hard to find the words to describe how I felt when I lost the person dearest to my heart. Even after all these years when I least expect it, that day creeps into my mind, uninvited. I hear Cammie's screams for help. I watch myself jump out of bed and stumble in a panic down the stairs.

"I relive every second of that bleak and dark day, but I stop my thoughts when I feel her wet dress clenched in my fingers so tightly. I can't let my memories go any further than that. It's my stopping point. Once you've lost your senses and somehow made it back, you realize how fragile your mind is. Yet the days and the years keep rolling by, and still, I long for her and miss her so.

"I wonder what she would have looked like at thirteen, or at twenty. Would she have fallen in love? What a lovely bride she would have made.

"These are the questions that I torture myself with. When I have a very bad day, I think of the grandchildren that I never had. What a wonderful and loving mother she would have been to them. Though they never existed, I still grieve for them. My regret is that I was never given the chance to be their grandmother.

"So you see, Danielle, though Isabella is gone from this life, she is always in my thoughts and close to my heart. She touched my life and changed who I was as a person. I will always miss her and I will always grieve for her."

At that point, Ms. Carine, put her trembling hand to her mouth. I saw one single tear fall from the corner of her eye. She smiled at me and continued her story from where she had left off previously.

"My doctor told me that Joshua did make visits to the sanitarium for a couple of years, and then the visits abruptly stopped. He continued to make payments for my care but never returned to visit me. They said my friend Bunetta came to see me a few times but I didn't recognize her and she left broken hearted.

"Eventually, the doctors and therapist began to work their way through the murkiness and the darkness in my mind. It was in one of my therapy sessions that my doctor confronted my new-found theory that God did not exist. He explained to me that if there was no God, then there could be no such thing as heaven or hell. He asked me if he was correct in his assumption?

"I nodded yes.

"He continued and said so when you die, it is finished; there is nothing more, and I again nodded yes. He looked at me with compassion and asked if I believed that Isabella wasn't in heaven and that she was still laying in that cold, hard ground. Is this really what I believed?"

"His statement sunk in and, I said, No, that can't be right, I have been wrong all of this time. What a fool I have been. Of course she is with God. Was my grief so deep, that I thought only of myself, not of her? The only hope I have is that one day I will see her again reunited in heaven.

"After that day, the healing process began. All of the anger holding me prisoner was set free. Forgiving my husband and myself made room in my heart for gratitude of the years that I had with her. I once again looked forward to our reunion in heaven.

"I was released from the asylum on a dark and dreary Monday. The asylum notified Joshua by letter to inform him of my homecoming. He didn't respond to my doctor's letter and no one was sent to pick me up. I could feel my doctor's pity as he accompanied me home.

"It was a welcome sight to see Rosa after all these years still here taking care of the household. My doctor informed me that a dear and old friend of Joshua's, name of Tate McGregor, had moved into the house after I was gone. Tate had died a couple of years earlier and had been buried in the family cemetery. How strange, I'd never heard of this man before. Where had he come from and why had I never met him? If he was such a close friend of my husband, why hadn't I been properly introduced to him? *And he was buried in the family plot?*

"All of the other servants had been let go when this Mr. McGregor moved in. It seemed that he was a mystery not only to me but to everyone else in the area. Could he be the secret that Joshua had been hiding from me and his family for all of those years? The missing pieces of the puzzle of Joshua's life started falling into place.

"The loveless and sexless marriage I had endured. The coolness of his touch on my arm and the nonchalant way he spoke to me. The endless nights he spent away from me year after year. All of that time, I thought it was another woman who had his heart. How wrong was I ! Ours was a marriage of convenience, not for me but for him.

"Ms. Carine, are you insinuating what I think you're are?" I asked, with a look of shock on my face.

"Yes, Danielle, I am. Those things happened, just as they do now. They just hid it better back then.

"Joshua came to Boston, looking for that perfect, naive and innocent little girl to snatch up and carry to the woods and dirty bayous' of Louisiana. What a little fool I was!

"How naive was I to not figure this secret out years ago! I thought of what Stella said to me, that I lived with my head in the sand. She knew. She had always known who her brother was. They both understood that sometimes secrets should be kept forever.

"My doctor was afraid that all of the memories would come rushing back to me when I came back home but he didn't have to worry. The years had dulled the pain in my heart, and in its place sadness had moved in. I would always love and grieve for my darling daughter. This would never change and I had accepted my loss.

"I missed her sweet smile and the lovely dimples in her cheeks. I missed the smell of her silky blond hair and the spark in her emerald green eyes. I could almost feel the weight of her body sitting in my lap and her hand stroking my face. I would never understand why she lost her life so young, but I had come to appreciate the years that God had given me to spend with her.

"When I first saw Joshua his appearance was shocking. He was thin and frail, just a shell of the man I remembered. He sat in the library gazing out the window and only glanced at me briefly like I had been gone for only a day instead of years. I was only home for a week when Joshua had a massive stroke and died in his chair. The thought crossed my mind that at least I was spared of having to care for him in his old age. My suffering had been profound but I had finally found God's favor. He was buried in our family cemetery next to Isabella as should be. I had peace knowing that one day I would be put to rest next to my dear little girl. I just don't understand why God hasn't taken me yet, I have been ready for so long."

"Maybe you were waiting to tell your story. Maybe you were waiting for me," I replied.

"Yes, that must be the reason why. I was waiting for you, Danielle, replied Ms. Carine. I want you to tell the world about our life here and how our families lived and survived on this land. Share our joy and our suffering with the people who come after us. Our lives had meaning and the things we accomplished mattered. Don't let us be forgotten as if we never existed.

"I've outlived every single person that I've ever known. Once I pass, no one will know that I ever existed, and they will never know how special Isabella was.

"When you lose a child you become a different person than who you once were. You become a mother without a child. Your role has changed and you don't know who you are anymore. It's easy to lose your purpose in life, I know because I lost mine. I guess that's why this is so important to me because if it's written down, someday, someone will read my story, and we will live again and give them hope. You're the last piece of the puzzle in my life coming together.

"Now, I'm tired, and I must rest. As I promised you, Rosa will take you upstairs to see Isabella's room and the rest of my house. Don't forget my words to you, and remember the things that I have taught you. I am leaving my legacy in your capable hands."

Ms. Carine closed her eyes and laid her head against the chair.

Rosa appeared at my side and said, "Come on, Ms. Danielle, here's what you been waiting on."

"I felt so shaky that I didn't know if I could make it up the stairs. My hands were numb from holding onto the rails so tightly. Rosa unlocked the door at the top of the stairs and swung it open. A rush of icy cold air hit me in the face, and I started shivering uncontrollably.

Rosa turned to face me and said, "I'll let you look around on your own. That room was Ms. Carine and Mr. Joshua's bedroom. The next one was Stella's and then it was Isabella's room. The other room belonged to Robert. Take your time looking around."

"And then she was gone. She just disappeared into thin air before my very eyes.

"My head was in a fog and everything was surreal. The upstairs was bleak and filthy with cobwebs hanging from the ceilings. The hardwood floors were dirty, dark, and scratched up. I opened the door to Ms. Carine's room first. In the bedroom was an old iron bed with a nightstand next to it, a dresser, and an old rocker. The curtains were dirty and torn and hung rotting from an old curtain rod.

"On the nightstand was a small picture of Ms. Carine and Isabella sitting in the swing with smiles on their faces. They were both so beautiful, and I could feel the love between them.

"I picked up the photo and put it in my pocket. As I walked around the bedroom the dirty floorboards creaked, and outside the winds blew while the old house groaned.

"I opened the door into her private bathroom that she was so proud of. I discovered that it was just a room with an old claw foot tub and toilet, nothing special to look at. But in her day, it was a luxury, and she had made this happen. It was important to her. As I walked out of the bathroom, the rocker in her bedroom started rocking slowly and I realized I was not alone.

"I started down the hall away from Ms. Carine's room. The hall was wide, and extremely dark. There were no windows in this hall, and the only light that entered was from the open doors of the bedrooms. The hall was painted the same sickly-green as the bathroom downstairs.

"I decided to enter Robert's room first, leaving Isabella's room for last. His room was simple, with just a single bed and an old armoire. The wallpaper was peeling off the walls, and they were bare except for a lone crucifix. The window panes were cracked and the air coming in was cold.

"Placed on the dresser was an old black and white snapshot of him sitting on the porch. He was looking at an older woman whom I figured was his mother, Mrs. Vernice. I wondered what had become of Robert, Ms. Carine had said very little of her brother-in-law.

"I steadied myself by holding onto the wall. How strange it was that Rosa just seemed to vanish right before my eyes! The air felt thinner up here, and it was difficult to breath.

"I slowly opened up the door to Isabella's bedroom. Her room had once been pretty. The walls were painted a cotton candy pink and there was an old dirty, flowered rug left on the floor. There was the window that I had seen the little girl looking out of the first time I came here. Beneath it was a small window seat, a wonderful spot to sit and read or play with her dolls.

"There were wooden shelves painted white, hanging on the wall with old books and a few small toys still sitting on them. The paint was peeling off the shelves, and the books had started to disintegrate.

"There was a very old doll sitting in the middle of the old iron bed. It felt like Isabella had played with the doll and left her on the bed only moments ago.

"Her bed was covered with a pink ruffled bedspread that had flowers on it. It was old and dirty. The colors in the flowers had long ago faded. This room had been left exactly as it was when Isabella was alive. There was a layer of dust, inches thick, covering everything and spider webs hanging from the ceiling. This room was the reason Ms. Carine did not want anyone upstairs.

"Picking up Isabella's doll I sat on her window seat. Right before my eyes, Isabella and Cammie materialized.

These two little girls were playing jacks on the floor, giggling and schussing each other to keep quiet. I saw her room as it once had been when she lived and played in it. Izzy was ordering

Cammie to be quite. Her mother was asleep, and she didn't want to wake her. Her mother must be feeling bad because she never napped.

"Deciding to go outside and play Isabella noted that it was unusual that none of the servants were around. The girls ended up at the pond, and Cammie said, "No one is around so let's get in and cool off. It's so hot today."

Izzy said, "I can't. I'm not allowed to go into the water. I don't know how to swim well, and mother forbids it."

"Cammie proceeded to take her shoes off. She sat at the edge of the pond and dropped her feet into the cool water. She screamed a little and said, "The water is so cold, Isabella. Come and put your feet in! Come on Izzy, take your shoes off. Your mother will never know."

Izzy looked up toward her mother's bedroom and thought about it. She quickly kicked her shoes off before she had time to change her mind. She stepped into the water and squealed with delight. For a brief moment, she felt brave and took another step.

"Come on in the water with me, Cammie, pleaded Isabella. It's not that cold once you get in."

Cammie said, "No, Izzy, don't go any further. Neither one of us can swim very well. Please don't go any further, or you will wet your dress. Your mother will find out, and we'll both get whipped."

"As Izzy turned to look at Cammie, her foot slipped into a hole. As she went underwater Cammie's mouth fell open in surprise waiting for Izzy to come back up, but she didn't. I saw the look of shock on Cammie's face as she realized what was happening and I watched in horror as the sounds of her screams woke Carine from her nap. In amazement I saw a much younger Carine running outside toward the pond, and then I saw Isabella's body floating under that dirty water.

"Instantly I was back in Isabella's room with all of the dirt and spider webs. The sun was going down, and I was suddenly afraid. Something wasn't right, but I couldn't put my finger on what it was.

"It occurred to me then that today was my birthday, and it was also the end of Ms. Carine's story. I slowly backed out of Isabella's room and called for Rosa.

"The hall was pitch black and I couldn't see where I was going. I felt a presence in that hall with me and the hair on my neck stood up. Again, I called out Rosa's name but my voice just echoed in the emptiness of the house.

"Touching the walls I hurriedly made my way in the darkness. Finally reaching the door to the staircase I turned to get one more look at the upstairs. It was then that I noticed Robert standing at the door to his bedroom. He looked at me with a lewd smile and started to unzip his pants. He then proceeded to walk towards me.

"Screaming loudly I grabbed the handle opening the door to go downstairs. I looked back, and he was right behind me. As his hand reached out to grab my shoulder he vanished into thin air.

"As I opened the door to the stairway, I gasped. The stairs were rotted away and there were only a handful of planks left to climb down. There was a gaping hole in the roof where a tree had fallen, and the house was decaying, falling in on itself. I screamed for Ms. Carine and then for Rosa but to no avail. There was no one here but me and the rats, as I watched them scurrying about.

"I made my way down the rotted staircase as best I could and wandered about the house, confused and lost. What had happened here? I was so dizzy it was difficult to walk. The house was in a state of decay, and just being in it was dangerous. I went into the library, and the windows were smashed, with glass scattered everywhere. Graffiti had been painted on the floors and the walls and someone had spray-painted "I Was Here!" on one wall in the library.

"As I walked into the kitchen, I noticed that the back door was missing from the hinges. The cabinet doors were either broken, hanging at an angle, or missing altogether.

"Someone had rummaged through them, and all of the glassware and crystal were gone. Vines were growing along the walls and nature had been busy reclaiming this space as its own.

"I walked out of the back door and made my way to the wrought iron fence. This fence had mystified and intrigued me since my first visit here. There was a full moon out tonight, and it was shining like a beacon on the headstones inside of the fence.

"I had to forcefully lift up and open the gate because it was stuck in the overgrown grass. This gate had not been opened in a very long time. There in the center of the cemetery was Isabella's grave. A statue of a weeping angel had been placed in front of it.

"Joshua was buried on one side of her and Ms. Carine on the other. Her tombstone read, "Herein lays Carine. May she be reunited with her beloved daughter, and may her soul find eternal rest." Carved into the headstone was the date of her death, March 25, 1920. Today was March 25, 1970. It was also my birthday. She had died fifty years ago on the very day that I was born. Was it possible that our souls touched one another as she passed through this world at the end of her life, just as I was being born into mine?

"How could this be happening? Nothing was making any sense. I visited with Ms. Carine every Saturday for the last six months. I ate with her, and had lengthy conversations.

She shared her life story with me. I couldn't make that up, could I? We were friends. It occurred to me that maybe I'd gone crazy because crazy people don't know they're crazy. What have I been doing all this time and with whom?

"I stumbled out of the cemetery and started to make my way to my car trying to make sense of what I had just seen. I turned around for one last look at the house that I had come to love.

Now I could see that it had been empty for many years and was decrepit. I looked toward the graveyard, and there was the little girl, walking and leading an old lady by the hand. They both turned around to look at me, and the little girl smiled.

It was only then that I recognized the little girl by her beautiful dimples. It was Isabella, and she was holding Ms. Carine's hand. Isabella had been waiting all of this time for her mother to take her hand so she could lead her into the light, so that they both could finally Rest in Peace. It was the message she was trying to convey to me all of these months.

"As I was turning to leave, out the corner of my eye, I saw a creature falling from the sky and swooping down behind them. The noise of the wings was so intense that I had to place my hands over my ears to try and drown the sound out. The wings on the creature shone like gold and when spread out, encompassed both Isabella and Ms. Carine. The creature slowly turned its head toward me. Its eyes burned with the intensity of a hot white fire.

"It lowered its head as if to nod to me and when its head raised up, there was a small smile on its glowing face. It was then that I recognized Rosa.

"She wasn't evil as I had believed her to be, after all. She was Carine's guardian angel, given to her at birth. She had stood by her side throughout her life and into her death. She was sent here to protect her.

"It was then that I understood that life is indeed a puzzle. Things that happen to you fall into place, one piece at a time. The last piece to fall into place will be your death. The circle of life is then completed, one person taken to make room for another person to be born.

"I remembered Ms. Carine's words, "If you live long enough, you start to put it all together."

"Yes, Ms. Carine, I understand and I am beginning to put it all together.

The End

ABOUT THE AUTHOR

Debby Lawson is a poet, photographer, writer and author of the new novel "And Time Stood Still". She describes herself as a late bloomer with an over active imagination that leans toward ghosts and the supernatural with a strong belief in guardian angels. She works as a legislative aid for the State of Louisiana and lives in South Louisiana with her husband Paul, their Weimarnar Charlie and their cat Thelma. She is currently working a sequel. You can reach Debby through her facebook blog, Debby Lawson "Write On".